M000307041

COLORADO COLD CASE

BROTHERHOOD PROTECTORS COLORADO BOOK #8

ELLE JAMES

TWISTED PAGE INC

COLORADO COLD CASE

BROTHERHOOD PROTECTORS COLORADO
BOOK #8

New York Times & USA Today
Bestselling Author

ELLE JAMES

Dedicated to my readers who let me write stories for them to love! Thank you!
Elle James

AUTHOR'S NOTE

Enjoy other military books by Elle James

Brotherhood Protectors Colorado
SEAL Salvation (#1)
Rocky Mountain Rescue (#2)
Ranger Redemption (#3)
Tactical Takeover (#4)
Colorado Conspiracy (#5)
Rocky Mountain Madness (#6)
Free Fall (#7)
Colorado Cold Case (#8)
Fool's Folly (#9)

Visit ellejames.com for titles and release dates
For hot cowboys, visit her alter ego Myla Jackson at
mylajackson.com
and join Elle James's Newsletter at
https://ellejames.com/contact/

PROLOGUE

"WHAT ARE WE WAITING ON?" John "Griff" Griffin murmured as he held his position and waited for the go-ahead from the team lead.

"What's your hurry?" Freddy "Mercury" Rodriguez answered. "Got a hot date back in the States?"

"Maybe," Griff admitted. *If she hasn't already forgotten I exist*, he thought.

"That black-haired, green-eyed beauty you met at McP's?" Merc asked.

"Maybe," Griff repeated. He didn't like to own up to having a thing for anyone. Their lives belonged to the Navy. It was foolish to think he could maintain a relationship, much less start one, when they were at the beck and call of the military.

As highly trained Navy SEALs, their lives weren't their own. Not as long as they stayed in the military.

He'd met her the last time his team had visited their favorite bar, McP's, in San Diego. They'd been on three dates before his team had gotten called up for a mission. He hadn't even had time to let her know he'd be gone or for how long. They never knew.

The longer they were away, the less likely she'd be around when he returned.

Trouble was…he liked this one. A lot.

"Let's get this operation over with already," Griff muttered.

"Hey, Griff, what's it look like on point?" JJ Roberts's voice sounded in Griff's headset.

Griff studied their target, the building at the center of the little village in Syria. "Quiet. Nothing moving, not even the guard in front of the target building. I think he's asleep."

"I count two sentries on the main road leading into the village, leaning with their backs against a couple of homes," JJ said.

"Got two on the other end of town, same situation. Leaning with their AK-47s slung across their bodies," Derek Badger's gravelly voice hummed in Griff's ear.

Griff's gut tightened. "Too easy," Griff said softly.

Peter "Crack" Weissmuller chuckled. "Only easy day was yest—"

"Yeah. Yeah," Fridge, their team leader, said. "Focus on the objective."

They were there to extract a US citizen being held for ransom by ISIS – the Islamic State.

The Black Hawk helicopter had dropped them on the other side of a hill to avoid alerting ISIS to their imminent arrival. After a quick hike up and over the hill, they'd made their way to the village.

The team of eight Navy SEALs was tasked with extracting the citizen and getting him out of the country. Alive. If that meant taking out a handful of ISIS bastards, then so be it. Preferably with no civilian casualties, as always.

The ISIS abductors had purposefully chosen a quiet village full of civilians to surround them.

Wading through homes with women and children was like walking through a field of landmines. They had to make certain they didn't set any off and create collateral damage that would be reported on Al Jazeera the next day with images of the bloody bodies of children to remind the natives why they should hate the US.

"Ready when you are, Griff," Fridge said. "We've got your six."

Griff glanced across at his sidekick, Merc, and nodded. While Griff provided cover, his teammate gave him a thumbs-up and took off toward the target building, rushing forward and hugging the shadows of the mud and brick homes. When he reached a house one building short of their destination, he stopped and waited for Griff to leapfrog to the corner across from him.

Griff glanced behind him.

Fridge and Marty Sorenson brought up their rear. Crack and William "Willy" Daniels moved in from the opposite direction while JJ and Badger covered the town entrance.

Armed with a submachine gun and a nine-millimeter Glock, Griff took out his KA-Bar knife and slipped silently up to the guard at the front entrance to the building.

The man, dressed in the black clothing of the ISIS rebels, let the strap on his Soviet-made PKM machine gun do the work of holding the weapon in front of him. He was so sleepy that he didn't see Griff approach, nor did he have time to call out a warning to anyone inside or nearby.

Griff quietly dispatched the guard and dragged him into the shadows. He removed the bolt from the machine gun and slipped it into his pocket, rendering it ineffective. It would not be used against them that night.

He gave Merc a "follow me" sign. "Going in," he whispered into his headset.

"Right behind you," Merc said.

Griff pulled his night-vision goggles down over his eyes, pushed open the front door and entered, his machine gun with a silencer in place leading the way.

Merc followed.

Crack and Willy would bring up the rear, with Fridge and Marty covering the building from the outside.

One by one, they cleared each room, the soft sound of silenced gunfire barely making enough noise to rouse the ISIS soldiers from their sleep.

By the time they reached the locked door at the rear of the building, they'd dispatched nine ISIS rebels with no resistance.

The last door had a padlock on the outside of the door.

Griff slid his night-vision goggles up. Merc aimed the beam of his penlight at the lock while Griff pulled the bolt cutter from where it was strapped to his back and made quick work of the master lock on the hasp.

With the lock gone, the door swung open. Mercury shined his flashlight into the dark room.

The stench hit Griff first.

A man lay on the floor beaten, bloody, covered in excrement and so filthy Griff wasn't sure the man was Joe Franklin, the nephew of Senator George Franklin. Was this the American they'd been sent to rescue?

Griff bent over the man and rolled him onto his back. "What's your name?"

The man groaned something unintelligible.

"Boys," JJ's voice sounded in Griff's ear. "We've got

company. Looks like a whole company of ISIS headed our way in a convoy of trucks."

"Name!" Griff said more urgently.

The man forced sound through swollen lips. "Joe."

"Good enough," Merc said. "Get him out of here."

"Wrap it, Griff," Fridge said. "We have a date with a helo I don't plan to miss."

Griff bent, forcing back his gag reflex, grabbed the man's arm and pulled him up over his shoulder in a fireman's carry.

The hallways were too narrow for Merc to help. Griff had to carry the man out on his own. He'd been beaten so severely that he couldn't help himself, and it was like carrying a dead man. One who moaned every time his ribs bounced against Griff's armor plating.

"I hope you're on your way out of the village," JJ said. "They're coming in fast."

Gunfire sounded.

"Who opened fire?" Fridge demanded.

"None of us," JJ answered. "They're firing into the air. I won't be able to hold them off for long."

"Don't try," Fridge said. "Get back and head for our extraction point."

Griff emerged from the building, straining beneath the man's weight on his back.

Merc trotted along beside him. "Let me help."

"Help by getting us out of this shit hole before all hell breaks loose," Griff said through gritted teeth.

"Crack and Merc, take point. Marty and I will have your backs," Fridge said. "Go!"

Crack and Merc led the way through the small village, heading back the way they'd come—not by the road leading in from north to south. They headed west toward the hill, on the other side of which the Black Hawk waited for the signal to fly in and extract the team and their target.

The quiet village was now a cacophony of gunfire and shouts.

Where they had met little resistance coming in, now, people stumbled out of homes, armed and ready to fight.

If they held a gun, Merc and Crack took them out before they could fire on them first.

Griff ran with a lumbering gait, weighed down by the man draped over his shoulder. Somewhere between bumping into walls and bouncing against what Griff suspected were broken ribs, Joe had passed out.

Ahead, between two mud and stick structures, Griff caught a glimpse of the open field beyond and the Black Hawk rising above the ridge.

All he had to do was get his burden to the middle of that field and onto the chopper. His goal clear, and his focus lasered in on the helicopter, Griff pushed himself harder, picking up speed.

He burst out into the open, still running, careful not to stumble over brush or rocks. If he went down, he wasn't sure the man he carried could take the fall. Hell, he wasn't sure he'd be able to get back up himself, much less collect Joe and get moving again. He'd do his best to stay on his feet and keep his forward momentum.

Merc and Crack fell back and covered for him as he charged toward the Black Hawk swooping toward him into the field.

Gunfire erupted behind him.

Griff didn't look back. When he got Joe on board, he'd turn and help the others. Until then, he had one job, and he'd damn well better get it right.

As the Black Hawk hovered above the field, the gunner hanging out the side door opened fire with his fifty-caliber machine gun.

Fuck. That meant the guys behind Griff were in trouble.

Griff kept moving, closing the gap to where the chopper was descending.

Finally, the bird was down. Ten yards. Just ten yards.

His shoulder, back and legs screaming from the weight, Griff rushed forward. The medic inside the craft grabbed Joe as Griff flipped him off his shoulder. Together they lowered him to the metal floor of the chopper.

As soon as Joe was down, Griff spun, swung his machinegun around and ran back toward the others.

Merc and Crack were only steps away. All three

turned and covered for Willy, JJ, Badger, Marty and Fridge as they emerged from the shadows of the village.

Not far behind, men in black poured from between the huts like so many ants streaming from a hive.

With the help of the helicopter's gunner, Griff, Merc and Crack fired on the ISIS rebels, forcing them back to the cover of the buildings.

Willy, JJ and Badger raced past Griff and leaped onto the chopper.

Marty and Fridge were the last to approach.

Marty went down less than five yards from Griff.

Fridge scooped him up, flung him over his shoulder and kept coming.

As soon as they passed him, Griff shouted to Merc and Crack. "Go! I'll cover."

The men backed toward the helicopter, continuing to fire as they did.

"Griff, get in!" Fridge yelled into Griff's headset. "This bird's gotta fly."

Griff turned and ran for the chopper, already lifting off the ground.

He dove for the door.

Hands reached out for him. He grabbed hold of Fridge and Merc's hands. Together, they pulled him up as the chopper rose into the air.

Griff's legs dangled in the air for several heart-stopping moments while the gunner rained fire onto the ISIS rebels below.

Fridge and Merc dragged him onto the chopper. All three men collapsed onto the floor, breathing hard.

"We're not out of the woods yet," Badger's voice sounded in Griff's radio headset.

Griff sat up in time to see a truck spinning out into the field they'd just left. It stopped, and a man leaped out, placed an RPG across his shoulder and fired.

"Incoming!" Badger called out.

A second later, the Black Hawk shuddered violently. Where the gunner had been was a gaping hole. The engine sputtered and died. The rotors slowed, and the entire craft plummeted to the earth.

The last thing Griff heard was Crack yelling, "Fuck!"

CHAPTER 1

RACHEL WEST'S phone vibrated on the nightstand for the second time in as many minutes. The first time it had rattled against the wooden stand, Rachel had barely surfaced from a dead sleep. The night shift as a California Highway Patrol officer was kicking her butt.

Midday was her sleep time. She'd turned off the sound on her cell phone to avoid spam callers trying to sell her siding for a house she didn't own or a service contract on her vehicle.

When the phone rattled against the nightstand so quickly after the first call, Rachel groaned and rolled over. Her fog-clouded mind perked up at the thought of getting a call from the hot Navy SEAL who hadn't contacted her in over a week. She glanced at her phone, hoping to see Griff's caller identification. It wasn't Griff.

Lindsay.

Rachel frowned. Her sister knew she was on the night shift and respected her sleep time. She wouldn't call unless it was necessary. "Hey, Lindsay."

"Rachel, talk to me," Lindsay said, her voice a little breathless.

"What's wrong?"

"I don't know," her sister answered. "I'm out on a hiking trail a few miles west of Fool's Gold. I think someone is following me."

Rachel sat up straight, her pulse kicking up. "Are you alone?"

"Yes, except for the guy following me."

Rachel's gut clenched. She'd warned her sister to always hike with a buddy. Twenty-three-year-old Lindsay still had the *it-won't-happen-to-me* mentality and wouldn't listen to reason. "Are you carrying a weapon?" she asked.

"No. I'm not licensed for concealed carry, nor can I get in a good hike packing a heavy gun."

"We discussed this," Rachel said. "What if you run into a bear or a wolf? That goes for the four-legged as well as the two-legged wolves."

"I know. I know. I just never run into either."

"Until you do."

"Yeah," Lindsay sighed. "Now, I'm wishing I'd taken your advice."

"Sweetie, is there any way you can circle back to your car?"

"No," Lindsay said. "The trail is steep. I have to go back the way I came."

"You should call 911. They'll use your cell phone location to find you."

"I don't want to hang up. I'm afraid that if I do, whoever is following me will use the time between calls to close the distance between us."

"Can you see him now?" Rachel asked. "Can you describe him?"

"No. He's staying just out of range. This trail is crazy curvy, zigzagging in and out of steep ravines. I was heading for a waterfall, but now, I just want to get back to my car."

Her pulse speeding, Rachel pressed her cell phone to her ear. "Stay on the phone with me. I'll go next door and see if my neighbor can call 911 for you."

"Don't hang up," her sister's voice shook.

Wishing she was there with Lindsay, Rachel could only do her best to get someone else to help. Someone closer to her sister in Colorado. "I'm not going to hang up." Rachel walked out the front door of her apartment, leaving the door unlocked. She walked to the next apartment and knocked sharply on the door. "Still with me?"

"Yes," Lindsay whispered. "I think he's getting closer. I just rounded a rocky bluff. I can't see on the other side, but I hear footsteps and the sound of gravel sliding over the edge."

"Drop a pin on your location and send it to me so I can send it to the authorities."

"I'll have to stop moving."

For a moment, Rachel heard nothing. "Lindsay?"

"There. I sent my location," Lindsay finally said, her voice so soft, Rachel could barely make out her words.

Rachel's cell phone gave the electronic sound of an incoming message. "Got it," she said, staring down at the pin on a map. "Be ready to snap a picture of the guy. It might make him think twice about doing anything stupid."

"I'm scared," Lindsay whispered.

"I'm with you, sweetie." Rachel knocked on the door again. "You know I love you."

"I haven't always said it, but I love you, too."

"Hang in there," Rachel said and moved on to the next apartment. "I have to try another door."

"Shh," Lindsay said. "Oh, shit. Oh, shit. I hear him. He's running toward me."

Rachel's heart slammed against her ribs. "Find a stick or a rock, something to use as a weapon."

"I have a rock. I can't outrun him. I'm going to turn and stand my ground."

"Be ready to Snap a photo of him and text it to me."

"Sweet Jesus, help me," Lindsay said, her voice farther away as if she held the phone away from her mouth.

14

Rachel pounded on the next door. "Please, I need help," she called out.

"He's here," Lindsay said. "Why are you following me?"

"Because you're mine," a voice said. It wasn't deep and resonant, but a kind of medium tone with no hint of an accent.

"No," Lindsay said. "I'm not yours. I don't even know you. So, move aside so I can get down off this trail."

The door in front of Rachel opened, and a man with scraggly gray hair scowled at her. "What do you want?"

"I need you to call 911."

His scowl deepened. "Why? You got a phone. Call them yourself."

"I'm on the phone with my sister. Someone is attacking her right now. I need you to help her." Rachel stared up at the man. "Please."

"Fine." He tipped his head toward his living room. "I'll call, but you'll have to do the talking. I don't know what you got going on."

Rachel clutched the phone to her ear. "Lindsay, if he attacks, you fight him with everything you've got."

"You shouldn't have run," the man's voice said over the phone.

"Run? You're creeping me out. You shouldn't be following me. I have a right to be on this trail. Get out of my way."

"No," he said, his tone ominous.

"Here." Rachel's neighbor handed her the cell phone. "I have 911 on the line."

Holding her cell phone to one ear and the neighbor's phone to the other, she said, "My sister is on a trail in Colorado, being attacked as we speak. I need someone to get out there before something terrible happens."

A scream sounded on her cell phone. Rachel's hand shook so hard that she fumbled with her cell phone and nearly dropped it. She let go of the other phone, and it dropped to the ground.

Her neighbor swore and retrieved the phone.

"Lindsay?" Rachel pressed her phone to her ear, stomach roiling, her heart pounding so fast and hard she could barely breathe.

The line had gone dead.

Rachel redialed her sister's number. It went directly to her voicemail.

She tried again with the same result. "Damn. Damn. Damn."

Rachel reached for the phone her neighbor held and redialed 911. After reporting her sister's attack, she ended the call. "Thank you," she said to her neighbor as she ran back to her apartment while speaking to her smartphone to call the sheriff's department in Fool's Gold, Colorado.

When she got through to the sheriff's department, she reported her sister's attack and sent the GPS location to the dispatcher's cell phone number. She gave her information for the sheriff to contact her when they found Lindsay.

Rachel didn't waste time. She searched for airline tickets to get from San Diego to Colorado Springs. Flights were completely booked for that day. The next available seat was on a plane leaving the following morning.

She booked the flight refundable in case her sister called back and said everything was fine. She prayed that would be the case and refused to think otherwise. Lindsay had probably dropped her phone while fighting off her attacker and was on her way back to her vehicle, uninjured and anxious to find a phone to let her sister know she was okay.

Her gut still knotted, Rachel got out her suitcase. Either way, she was going to Colorado to talk her sister into moving home to San Diego. Hiking alone in the mountains was just plain stupid. When she saw Lindsay again, she'd shake some sense into her.

After she hugged her and told her how much she loved her.

Lindsay was her only family. Though they'd shared a mother, they had different fathers. Rachel's had disappeared shortly after Rachel had been born, leaving her mother to raise her daughter alone. When Rachel was four, her mother met and married Jim Stratton, the love of her life. Lindsay's father became the only father Rachel ever knew and loved.

Lindsay was born a year after their mother married Jim. Rachel loved her beautiful little sister and their perfect family.

When Rachel went off to college, she came home for holidays until the day she got the call that her mother and stepfather had been killed in an automobile accident.

She'd come home immediately to be with Lindsay. Never had she doubted that she could support Lindsay and raise her to adulthood. Their parents had left them the house, which had been paid off through mortgage insurance. Rachel hired on with the California Highway Patrol as a cop to pay the bills and put food on the table.

It had been Rachel and Lindsay against the world from that point until Lindsay had graduated college and decided to explore the country. She'd made it as far as Fool's Gold, Colorado, where she'd fallen in love with the Rocky Mountains.

Rachel had been heartbroken when Lindsay had decided to stay in Colorado. She'd thought her sister just needed time to see other places and would eventually come home to California.

She packed underwear, long-sleeved shirts, jeans and a jacket in the suitcase. For a long moment, she stood staring at a picture of her and Lindsay laughing in the sun on a beach in San Diego a few years ago.

Tears welled in Rachel's eyes.

"Please, be okay," she whispered to the photo. "Please."

Over the next hour and a half, she packed, repacked and called her supervisor to say she'd be out for at least a few days. Then she paced the floor a hundred times, anxious to hear news but dreading it at the same time.

Finally, her phone chirped.

Rachel raced to pick it up, expecting to hear her sister's voice. Praying for it.

"Ms. West, this is Sheriff Faulkner from Fool's Gold, Colorado."

Her heart sank to the bottom of her belly.

"My deputies and I responded to your request to check on your sister's coordinates on a trail west of town."

Please be okay. Dear Lord, please let my sister be okay, Rachel prayed silently.

"We found her—"

"Is she okay?" Rachel blurted. "Please tell me she's okay."

The sheriff's pregnant pause sucked the air out of Rachel's lungs.

"I'm sorry to inform you that we found your sister unresponsive."

Rachel fell to her knees. As a patrol officer with the California Highway Patrol, she knew what unresponsive meant.

"Do you have someone who can be with you, Ms. West?" the sheriff asked.

"Nobody," she whispered. "Lindsay was my only relative."

"I'm so sorry for your loss," the sheriff said. "She's been taken to the medical examiner for a full autopsy."

Tears slipped from Rachel's eyes and streamed down her face. "I wasn't there. I could do nothing."

"She was a mile up the trail," the sheriff said. "We couldn't get there fast enough to save her. I've given the medical examiner your number so you can work out the details of her disposition. I know it's a lot to process. If you need anything, you can always call me later."

"I'm flying to Colorado Springs tomorrow," Rachel said, her voice shaking on suppressed sobs.

"I'll be here in Fool's Gold," he said, "to answer any questions you might have."

"How—" Rachel swallowed past the lump in her throat. "How did she die?"

"The medical examiner will have to complete a full examination. But from what I could see, she was strangled to death with what appears to be a wedding veil."

Anger burned through her veins, pushing past the tears. "The killer?"

"At large."

Her hand tightened around the cell phone. "Any clues as to who he is?"

"None," the sheriff said. "He didn't leave even a footprint behind."

"Did you locate my sister's cell phone?" Rachel asked.

"No," he answered. "The state crime scene investigators conducted a thorough search of the area. He was thorough to the point he used something to brush away his footprints."

"Thank you for letting me know," Rachel said. "Calls like this aren't easy."

"I'm sorry about your sister," the sheriff said. "I want you to know we're working the case and hope to find some leads."

"Thank you. I'll see you tomorrow." Rachel ended the call. Unable to do anything to make her world better, she buried her face in her hands and gave in to her grief.

That night she cried all the tears she would allow.

After that, she wouldn't wallow in self-pity anymore. Not when her sister's murderer was still out there. She'd find him and bring him down if it was the last thing she did.

For Lindsay.

CHAPTER 2

Six months later...

GRIFF SLOWED his truck to make the turn off the highway onto the country road deep in the heart of the Rocky Mountains of Colorado. He'd spent the past month selling the few pieces of furniture he'd accrued over the years, donating what he didn't plan to take and packing what personal items he cared to keep and that fit in the back of his truck.

After eleven years in the US Navy, he didn't have much to show for his life and didn't really care. Things were replaceable.

People weren't.

He couldn't replace the seven members of his team that hadn't survived the crash landing that had also killed the pilots, the gunner and the man they'd been sent to rescue. All in all, eleven of the twelve men on board that Black Hawk had died.

Griff, the sole survivor, had been thrown clear of the fuselage before it had hit the ground and burst into a fiery ball of flame fed by half a tank of aviation fuel meant to get them back to the relative safety of their forward operating base.

All Griff had suffered was a compound fracture to his left leg, a dislocated shoulder and a concussion.

When he'd come to, the helicopter had been a mass of fire, lighting up the sky. Even if he could have run to it, he couldn't have saved anyone inside.

As he'd watched from thirty yards away, the ISIS rebels had gathered around the burning hull, firing their weapons into the air, shouting and laughing at what they'd accomplished.

Fighting the fog of semi-consciousness, Griff had used his good arm to drag himself away from them and had hidden behind a boulder where he'd succumbed to the pain of his broken leg and the loss of his friends and brothers in arms.

Now, after months of rehabilitation and being medically retired from the Navy, he was on his way to what he hoped wasn't his next big mistake.

Stone Jacobs, an old friend from BUD/S training, had come to see him in Bethesda, where he'd spent most of his time in rehab, getting back as much mobility out of his damaged leg as he could. Stone had heard he was being released from his commitment to the Navy by the medical review board.

Though his leg was repaired, it would never be the same. He'd never pass the physical fitness tests required of a Navy SEAL, nor would he want to be in a position where a team member was relying on him to move quickly. No, his Navy days were over.

Not that he wanted to go back to the job. Not after losing his entire team. The only one to survive, he'd also had to answer to the US senator whose nephew had died in that crash as well. Not only had he lost his team, he'd failed in his mission to extract Joe Franklin from the hands of ISIS and return him to the States alive.

He should have died in the crash along with his team. At least then, he would have died a hero, not live on as the lone survivor of a failed mission. He didn't care about being a hero. He didn't care to live after his teammates had all perished.

So many times over the past six months of pain, he'd asked himself *Why me?*

Why had his life been spared and the others not?

He sighed and pressed his foot to the accelerator. His heart was not in the meeting he was going to have with Stone Jacobs at the Lost Valley Ranch just outside of Fool's Gold, Colorado.

What good could he bring to the Brotherhood Protectors, the brainchild of the legendary Hank

Patterson, another Navy SEAL whose exploits and successes were stuff legends were made of?

He'd promised to at least meet with Jacobs and Patterson before he told them he wasn't interested. They'd paid for the gas he'd used to get from San Diego, where he'd cleared out his apartment.

He hadn't had a single call, note or text from Rachel West, the woman he'd been so focused on before their operation had gone to shit. Hell, he hadn't wanted to see her or anyone when he'd come back. He'd wanted to forget he'd ever existed.

If not for the cleanup crew who'd come looking for the bodies of his team, he would have died where he laid behind the rock. And he should have. But they hadn't given up. They'd had a certain number of bodies to retrieve, and, by God, they'd looked until they'd found him, unconscious, hiding like a coward behind a rock.

Griff stared at the road ahead, slowly picking up speed. The sooner he got this meeting over, the sooner he could be back on the road.

To where?

He didn't have a home. His folks had died in a freak boating accident his first year in the Navy. He'd relied on his team to be his family. Now, they were dead.

And it was getting late.

He'd left Colorado Springs before dusk. The road through the pass had been crowded with people going home from work. Dusk had dropped over the mountains as soon as the sun slipped past the peaks.

Now, with little light remaining in the sky, he drove the curvy road toward the Lost Valley Ranch.

As he rounded a bend in the road, he spotted an SUV in front of him heading in the same direction.

A four-wheeler burst from the woods in front of the SUV and passed directly in front of the swiftly moving vehicle.

Griff's foot hit the brakes on his truck as the SUV swerved sharply, drove off the road into a ditch and flipped over, landing upside down.

His heart pounding, Griff sped up and came to a screeching halt on the shoulder, his headlights aimed at the overturned vehicle. He punched the hazard lights button on his dash, grabbed a flashlight from the glove box and leaped out of the truck.

He slipped and slid down the embankment, pain shooting through his bad leg with every jolt. Griff straightened as he reached the bottom where the SUV lay, its wheels in the air, smoke pouring from its engine. The acrid scent of gasoline filled the air. He had to get the driver out. Quickly. If the SUV caught fire...

His gut clenched, and an image of the Black Hawk engulfed in flames nearly sent him to his knees.

The top of the SUV was caved in several inches, the driver's side window shattered. When he shined the flashlight at the window, the broken shards reflected the light, making it impossible for him to see inside.

"Hey, are you okay?" he called out. He held his breath, praying the driver had survived.

A woman's voice sounded. "I think so. I'm just hanging upside down by my seatbelt. The buckle won't release, and I can't find my quick release tool."

"Cover your eyes. I'll clear the glass."

He gave her a moment to shield her face and then used the other end of his flashlight to knock away the broken shards of the driver's door window. Once he'd cleared all the glass, he shined his light in through the open window.

The woman hung from her seatbelt, her long dark hair blocking his view of her face as she fumbled with the buckle.

"It's stuck," she said, her voice strained.

"Hold onto something. I'll cut it with my knife. But be ready. As soon as I do, you'll fall."

"The sooner, the better," she murmured. "The shoulder strap is digging into me. It tightened so much upon impact, I can barely breathe."

He dropped to his knees, wincing at the pressure on his bad leg. He propped the flashlight against the doorframe, aiming up at her. What he could see of her face through the veil of hair was covered in blood. Once he was in position, he said, "Hanging in there?"

She snorted. "I've got nowhere else to go." She

braced her hands against the upside-down roof of the SUV. "I don't have much to hold onto."

"I'll lean into you to ease your descent." Griff pulled his pocketknife from his jeans pocket, opened it and pushed his broad shoulders into the opening.

Dark hair dangled into his face. He shoved it aside and slipped the knife's blade beneath the shoulder strap, careful not to poke it into her breast.

"On three," he said. "One...two...three." He sliced through the belt with his razor-sharp knife blade.

She held her upper body steady, the belt across her hips keeping her from falling.

He leaned his shoulder into her and sliced at the belt across her lap.

Freed of constraint, her body crashed down on Griff's shoulder, the pain reminding him of his own previous injuries. He dropped the knife out of the way to avoid stabbing her and eased from beneath her and out of the SUV, allowing her to slip down to the roof of the vehicle below her. Once she was still, he reached inside and gripped her beneath her arms. "Can you wrap your arms around my neck?"

"I think so." She worked her arms out from beneath her, wrapped them around his neck and held on.

He pulled her free of the SUV, knocking the flashlight over in the process. Still on a steep slope, he couldn't push to his feet. Instead, he leaned back, dragging her out and across his body.

"Are you all the way out?" he asked, her breasts pressed to his chest, her hair hanging in his face. The darkness made it nearly impossible to see what was going on.

She moved her legs. "Yes. I'm out."

"Are you injured—arms, legs, internal, anything that you can tell?" he asked before he tried to move her any further.

"Just where the shoulder strap bruised me, and I think I hit my head on the steering wheel."

"Okay. I'm going to roll you onto your side. Don't try to jump up. With a head injury, you might get dizzy, fall and compound your injuries."

"Okay. But we should move quickly. I smell gas and smoke."

"On three," he said.

She tightened her hold around his neck. "Just roll."

He did until they both lay on their sides. The stars had yet to fill the sky with enough light to illuminate the crash scene. Her face was a pale blur with streaks of drying blood marring her features.

He pushed to his feet. "Can you stand?"

"Yeah," she said. "At least, I think I can."

He bent, draped one of her arms over his shoulder and slid his arm around her waist. "It's a slippery slope and steep, but the sooner we get clear of the vehicle, the better."

"Then let's go."

Pushing past the pain in his leg, he guided her up the embankment, sliding backward several times until they reached the road above.

Once there, she leaned into him. "Wow. I must have hit my head harder than I thought." Her words faded, and her knees buckled.

If Griff hadn't been holding her around her waist, she'd have dropped to the ground.

He scooped her into his arms and carried her the rest of the way to his truck. He fumbled with the door handle, finally getting it open. Then he placed her in the passenger seat, leaned the chair back and strapped her into her seat belt.

As he did, her eyes blinked open. She tried to sit up, but he placed a hand on her shoulder. "Lay still. We need to get you to a hospital."

She shook her head and winced. "No. I was on my way to see a friend. I'd rather go there."

He shook his head. "You've suffered head trauma. You could have a concussion or bleeding on the brain."

She sighed and closed her eyes. "Okay. If you insist. Though I feel fine, except for this splitting headache. And maybe I have a concussion. I swear I'm seeing things. Don't I know you?" She opened her eyes and frowned up at him. Then her eyes widened. "Griff?"

Now that he could see her in the light from inside his truck, he brushed her hair away from her bloody cheek and stared down into familiar green eyes. The voice, the black hair and green eyes … but not here. That's what confused him. He hadn't expected to find her here in Colorado. He was more accustomed to this face back in San Diego. "Rachel?"

She nodded and then shook her head. "I never expected to run into you here."

"I was going to say the same thing," he said. "What the hell?"

"No kidding." She laughed and winced. "Can we get me to the little hospital they have in Fool's Gold? I could use some pain relief. Then we can sort out how we came to be in the same place at the same time."

He closed her door and hurried around to slip into the driver's seat. Griff shot a glance her way as he made a U-turn and continued to Fool's Gold.

She lay quietly in the seat beside him.

Griff alternated between joy and despair at seeing the woman he'd been thinking about before his world and the helicopter had crashed around him.

"Why are you in Colorado?" she asked, her eyes still closed, her face pale.

"I was on my way to interview for a job," he said, his lips pressing into a tight line. The last time he'd seen her, he hadn't needed a job. He'd been an elite Navy SEAL and damn proud of it.

Rachel turned to look at him, her eyes searching

his face. "I thought you were committed to life in the Navy."

He couldn't face her, though he could see her frown from the corner of his eye. He forced a shrug. "Things change. I'm out and need to be gainfully employed."

"Where were you going for your interview, and why so late?" she asked.

"I was on my way to Lost Valley Ranch to interview for a position with the Brotherhood Protectors."

Rachel chuckled and winced. "Well, isn't today just full of coincidences?" Her lips twisted into a wry grin. "I was on my way to Lost Valley Ranch to ask for help from those Brotherhood Protectors."

He shot a quick glance in her direction. "Seriously?"

She nodded and pinched the bridge of her nose. "A lot has happened since our—" she paused, "since the last time I saw you."

Griff wanted to say *No shit* but nodded instead. "We can catch up later. Right now, we need to get you checked out and file a report about the four-wheeler driver. He could have gotten you killed. And he didn't bother to stop and render assistance."

She snorted. "I doubt he would. I have a sinking feeling he's part of the problems I've encountered since moving here over three months ago."

"You live here?" Griff's hands tightened on the steering wheel.

"I do now. I had nothing keeping me in San Diego, and I needed to be here more."

Griff turned onto Main Street. He'd been back in the States well before her move to Colorado. Granted, he'd been in Bethesda, Maryland, working to regain mobility. Still, he could have called her.

But he hadn't. She didn't need the burden of a broken man. She deserved a man who was whole, fit and mentally stable.

That man wasn't Griff. Not since the crash.

He slowed where the road ended in a T-junction in Fool's Gold and turned left onto Main Street. The Mountain Medical Clinic was on the corner, lights on inside. Griff pulled into the emergency entrance, shifted the truck into park and climbed down. "Stay here. I'll be right back."

She raised a hand and waved weakly, her eyes still closed. "Not going anywhere on my own."

Griff hurried through the door.

A woman looked up from the reception desk. "May I help you?"

"I need a gurney, a wheelchair or something. I have someone in my truck who was injured in an automobile accident."

The woman leaped from her seat. "Is he conscious?" She waited for his answer.

"Hopefully, but I won't know until I get back out to her."

"I'll get one of the orderlies to bring a gurney out to you."

"Great. I'll be outside waiting with her." Griff spun and rushed back out to his truck. He'd been gone a minute, maybe two. A short amount of time, but too long for his comfort. A person could die that quickly.

His heart racing, blood thumping through his veins, he yanked open the door and stared down at Rachel.

She lay still, her face so pale, and her breathing barely making her chest rise.

Panic threatened to overwhelm Griff. He touched her shoulder gently. "Rachel," he said softly.

A second passed, and another.

A little louder this time, he said, "Rachel."

Her eyes blinked open, and she stared up at him. "What? Do I look that bad?" Her lips curled up at the corners, and she closed her eyes again. "I must. You look scared."

Letting go of the breath that had lodged in his lungs, Griff smiled. "You look amazing for someone who just survived a wreck."

"Liar." She opened her eyes, her lips twisting. "Now, I know seatbelts work." A slight smile made her mouth widen. "I've always wondered."

"Come on," Griff said. "Let's get you inside." Unwilling to wait a moment longer, he unbuckled her belt and scooped her into his arms.

She draped an arm over his shoulders. "You really know how to sweep a girl off her feet."

He carried her toward the door. "Good thing that's all it takes to impress you." Taking it slowly, he tried not to limp, but he couldn't help it.

Her brow furrowed. "Did you hurt yourself rescuing me?"

He shook his head. "Old injury."

"Put me down. I'm sure I can walk on my own two feet."

The sliding glass doors opened, and an orderly pushed a gurney through the opening.

"Ah, your chariot has arrived."

"Seriously?" Rachel's frown deepened. "A wheelchair would've sufficed. Or I could've walked myself in. I'm not a pansy-ass female who can't take care of herself."

He settled her on the gurney and stepped back while the orderly moved the side rails up into position.

She glared. "Not liking this. The rails make me feel like a child in a playpen."

"A cute child," Griff said.

"Hospital rules," the orderly said. "When we're moving, the rails go up."

"It's okay," Griff said, a smile tugging at his mouth at her stubbornness. "Let the doc check you out. If he gives the all-clear, I'll spring you from this joint, and we'll be on our way to our mutual destination." He winked. "For now, play nice before they inject you with a sedative."

"They wouldn't do that." Rachel half-sat up, giving the orderly a narrow-eyed glare. "Would they?"

The orderly grinned. "I can't say. I'm not the doctor. Now, ma'am, if you'll just lie back, we'll get you into an examination room."

Griff was happy to see Rachel showing a little more pluck. He walked on the other side of the gurney until they reached the door marked Authorized Entry Only.

The orderly slid his ID over a card reader, and the door opened. He paused. "Sir, are you a relative?"

"No, but I did pull her from the vehicle."

His grin fading, the orderly shook his head and pushed the gurney through the door. "I'm sorry, sir. You'll have to wait in the lobby."

Griff started to follow, but the orderly stood in his way.

"He's not a relative *yet*," Rachel blurted from behind the man in white scrubs. "Does fiancé count?"

The orderly's frown flipped back to his easy grin. "Yes, of course. If he's your fiancé, he can go back with you." He tipped his head, indicating Griff could follow.

The man pushed the gurney past a couple of examination rooms, stopping at the third one on the right, next to the nurses' station. He set the brake on the gurney and backed out of the room. "I'll get the nurse."

Before he could turn, a nurse appeared in the doorway with a smile. "Hi, I'm Cristine. I'll be helping you today. What have we got here?"

"Automobile accident," Griff said. "We need a doctor to check her over."

The nurse asked questions, took her vital signs and entered the data into an online chart. Then she smiled at Rachel. "You're the new deputy in town, aren't you?"

Rachel nodded.

Griff's brow dipped, but he kept his comments and his own questions to himself until the nurse left the room, promising to be back with the doctor.

After the nurse left the room, Griff asked, "What happened to your job with the California Highway Patrol?"

She looked past him at the wall. "I resigned and took a position with the sheriff's department here."

"Isn't that like taking a demotion?"

Rachel lay with her dark, tangled hair fanning around her face on the white sheets. "Cost of living is slightly less than in San Diego."

"From what I remember, you loved your job there."

Her lips formed a thin line across her face. "Sometimes, you do what you have to do. This is one of those times."

Griff wanted to ask more questions. He opened his mouth, but before he could ask why, a doctor in a white coat entered the room, pulling a penlight from his pocket. "I hear you tried driving your car upside down." He grinned at his own joke. "How did that work for you?"

Rachel snorted. "Not so great."

The doctor nodded. "They work better on their wheels. Can you show me everywhere that hurts on you?"

She listed her ribs, shoulder and head.

The doctor listened to her chest and shined a pen light into her eyes. He pushed the skin around the gash on her forehead and stood back. "I'd like to keep you overnight for observation."

"Nope," Rachel said. "I'm fine. Only a headache and a couple of boo-boos."

"You show signs of a mild concussion. If you have a brain bleed, being in a hospital could save your life."

"Fine," Rachel laid back, crossing her arms over her. "But just one night. I have a job to do, and I need to meet with Mr. Jacobs to get some help."

"Speaking of Stone Jacobs," Griff said, "I should step out into the hallway and give them a call. Were they expecting you?"

"Yes. I was supposed to be there over an hour ago. Then everything went to hell, and here I am." She gave him a weak grin.

"And you're going to be back to normal in a day or so," Griff reassured her.

"I can't take off work," Rachel shook her head. "The sheriff's department is already short-staffed."

"Can't have a sheriff's deputy answering calls and passing out, can we?" the doctor said. "I'd give you a sedative to calm you, but it's not advisable with head injuries."

"I don't want one, anyway. I don't like it when I can't think clearly." She pinched the bridge of her nose again. "However, I could use something for this headache."

"I'll have the nurse bring you something for the pain. While we're waiting to get you assigned to a room for overnight observation, she'll clean your wound and apply a butterfly bandage to help it heal properly. I suggest you drive your car right-side up next time."

The doctor left the room.

Rachel sat up on the bed and swung her legs over the side.

Griff was at her side immediately. "Going somewhere?"

"I'd like to see the damage in a mirror." She scooted to the edge of the bed and slid off.

Once again, her knees buckled.

Griff caught her as she slid toward the floor. He hauled her up and held her close to his body. "Sweetheart, not that I mind holding you close, but you

39

really need to give yourself a break and rest. You've been through a helluva ordeal. Your body needs time to recuperate."

She pressed her hands to his chest. "I'm fine. I just didn't judge my distance to the ground well enough." When she pushed against him, he held steady for a moment then released her.

Rachel swayed and then seemed to get her balance. "See? I'm standing fine on my own."

"Until your next step." He shook his head. "He's not keeping you because you're weak at the knees. The doctor wants to ensure you don't have any swelling on the brain."

She stared up at him. "At least let me go to the sink and wash the dirt and dried blood off my face."

He nodded. "As long as you let me come along."

She shrugged. "I have no objections." Rachel crossed the room slowly and stopped in front of the sink, over which hung a small mirror.

Rachel glanced at her reflection and blinked. "Whoa. You could've told me I looked like something from the zombie apocalypse."

Griff grinned. "Prettiest zombie I've ever encountered."

Pulling several paper towels from the dispenser, she turned on the faucet, ran cool water over the paper towels and wiped them across cheeks, forehead and neck.

Careful not to disturb the gash on her forehead, she left the treatment of that injury to the nurse.

The nurse entered the room carrying a tray filled with gauze pads, scissors, bandages and more. When she spotted Rachel at the sink, she clucked like a mother hen. "You should be off your feet. If you fall, you'll injure yourself even more."

"Yes, ma'am." Rachel returned to the bed and planted her bottom on the edge of the mattress.

Griff helped her the rest of the way up.

While Rachel was still in a sitting position, the nurse spread out a pad on the pillow. She nodded toward Griff.

Griff helped ease Rachel downward until she lay on the bed.

"All this fuss over a little bump on the head," Rachel grumbled. "I'd like to give the bastard on the four-wheeler a bump."

"Did you get a good look at him?" Griff asked.

"No," Rachel said. "He wore a black helmet and moved so fast I couldn't even see the color of his ATV."

Nurse Cristine worked on cleaning the wound. Once she was done, she applied a butterfly bandage and then handed Rachel a pill cup and a Styrofoam cup filled with ice water.

Griff helped her sit up.

Rachel dutifully drank the water, washing down

the pill. Then she lay back against the pillow and closed her eyes.

Griff studied her for a long moment while she wasn't aware of what he was doing.

Throughout the doomed operation and the months of rehab he'd endured, he'd fought through the pain and uncertainty so that he could return to San Diego...to her. When he'd finally returned, he hadn't been able to force himself to call Rachel's number. He still had nightmares and woke up in a cold sweat.

She deserved a man who wasn't broken, damaged and not in a good place in his head.

"Will you stay put while I make that phone call?" he asked.

She cracked an eyelid. "Don't you trust me?"

He shook his head. "Not for a minute. Promise not to move?"

She sighed and closed her eyes again. "I promise."

Griff started for the door.

"Griff?" she called out softly.

He turned.

She was staring at him. "How long have you been back in the States?"

"Almost six months," he admitted.

The hurt in her eyes sank into his gut.

"Why didn't you call me?" she asked, looking small and vulnerable against the sterile white sheets.

He turned away. "I couldn't."

"Couldn't or wouldn't?" she persisted.

"Both," he said and stepped out into the hall, letting the door swing closed behind him.

He hadn't called because he wasn't the same man who'd left six months ago. Rachel hadn't changed. She was still beautiful and tough, yet vulnerable.

Every fiber of his being yearned for what could have been and would never be.

CHAPTER 3

RACHEL LAY in the hospital bed, feeling sorry for herself. Not because she was injured, but because Griff hadn't called her in the six months since she'd last seen him. And it wasn't like he'd been on a deployment.

Based on his answer as to why he hadn't called her, Rachel concluded Griff hadn't *wanted* to call. No excuses, no long, drawn-out goodbyes. He'd more or less ghosted her. What made her feel sorry for herself was that she'd felt a real connection with the Navy SEAL. She'd thought they'd formed an instant bond over thin and crispy pizza and beer.

Granted, she hadn't attempted to call him since a week after their last date. She'd asked around at McP's only to discover the team had been deployed. Where? She had no clue. That information was classified and given only to those with a need to know.

After her one attempt to call him, she'd received the call from Lindsay.

That night, her world had turned more upside down than she'd been in the crashed SUV. At least in the SUV, she'd been able to escape the horror.

Every day Lindsay's killer walked free, the terror continued.

The murderer had been labeled the Wedding Veil Killer. When the news agencies had caught wind of the moniker, they'd announced it over every news station and outlet in Colorado. The story had even made national news.

Rachel had flown out the next day to positively identify her sister's body and make arrangements to have her cremated. What use was a grave? Her sister was gone.

A visit to the sheriff's department in Fool's Gold had netted nothing. They had nothing to give. They were just as frustrated as Rachel.

She'd flown back to San Diego and worked another three months while constantly in contact with Sheriff Faulkner to the point he'd suggested she come to work for him and his understaffed department.

She'd taken him up on the offer and moved to Fool's Gold, determined to keep the town safe and find her sister's killer.

The murder had occurred six months ago. No

new clues had surfaced. No witnesses had come forward.

Lindsay's fiancé, Bryan Peterman, had been questioned on multiple occasions. He'd been harassed by reporters, targeted by vigilantes and forced to shutter his windows and work from home to avoid being harassed. Rachel wasn't completely convinced he was or wasn't the killer. She had no idea.

Her gaze on the door to her room, she willed Griff to walk back into the room. For the three months she'd lived in Fool's Gold, she'd never felt as safe as she felt with Griff. He'd pulled her from the wreckage in more ways than one.

She needed him. Too bad he didn't need her in his life.

The door swung open. The man foremost in her thoughts entered, tucking his cell phone into his jeans pocket. "Jake and Hank are on their way. I called the sheriff's department and reported the ATV driver, for what it was worth."

"There are so many ATVs in this area, it will be impossible to find that particular vehicle and driver."

"Especially if he doesn't want to be found." Griff crossed the room and took her hand in his. "I saw it happen. He almost killed you." He squeezed her hand gently then lifted it to his lips and pressed a kiss into her palm.

Rachel's heart swelled. She could fall in love with

this man. She'd been well on her way to doing just that when he'd deployed, and she'd lost her sister.

Despite the fact she knew he didn't feel the same way, she couldn't pull her hand free. She didn't want to. It felt like it was where it belonged.

The door burst open, and Sheriff Jim Faulkner entered like a freight train coming down a mountain pass. "West, what the hell? Why did I have to get a call from dispatch that you were in the hospital?"

"Sorry, sir," she said. "My cell phone is somewhere in my wrecked SUV, or I would've called you myself. I've been otherwise busy." She pulled her hand from Griff's grasp and gave her boss a crooked grin. "The bad news is that my SUV is totaled."

The sheriff's face softened. "The good news is you're going to be okay. I spoke with the doctor on my way down the hallway. But you're on leave until you're fully recovered."

Rachel frowned. "I can be back to work tomorrow, sir."

"Like hell," Griff and the sheriff said as one.

"Okay, so maybe the next day. I'm just bruised and have a knot on my head. It's not like I broke anything."

"You're lucky you got out that lightly." The sheriff shook his head. "You flipped your SUV?"

Rachel's lips pressed into a thin line. "It was all I could do to miss the ATV rider. He came out of nowhere and crossed right in front of me."

The sheriff shook his head. "Damned teenagers don't know what the hell they're doing."

"Yeah," Griff said. "And he didn't stop to render aid. He had to know he caused her to swerve off the road. The sound of the crash was loud enough to hear over the roar of an ATV engine."

Sheriff Faulkner frowned at Griff.

Griff held out his hand. "John Griffin," he said. "You can call me Griff."

"And you are...?" Frowning, the sheriff gripped the SEAL's hand.

"I was first on the scene. I saw what happened and pulled over as soon as Rachel's SUV left the road and rolled into the ditch."

"Thank you for saving one of my best deputies." The sheriff gave Griff's hand a firm shake and released it.

"I've only been a deputy for a few months," Rachel reminded him.

"Yeah, but your experience as a highway patrolman is far more valuable than the guys who come to me straight out of high school." The sheriff glanced from Rachel to Griff and back to Rachel. "I get the feeling you two know each other."

Rachel grinned. "We met in San Diego. Griff is a Navy SEAL."

The sheriff's brows rose. "Is that so?" He faced Griff.

"Former Navy SEAL," Griff corrected. "I separated from the Navy a month ago."

The sheriff's eyes narrowed. "You wouldn't happen to want a job as a sheriff's deputy, would you?"

Rachel chuckled.

"Thank you, sir. I actually came to Fool's Gold to interview for a position with the Brotherhood Protectors," Griff said.

The sheriff shook his head. "Well, damn. We can't compete with them. Not that we even try. They help us out when we're in a pinch, so I can't begrudge them some of the best recruits."

"Hey," Rachel said, "and I'm chopped liver?"

"I happen to love chopped liver," Sheriff Faulkner said with a grin. "And you're every bit as essential to our law enforcement team as anyone can imagine."

Rachel nodded. "That's more like it. I don't work for peanuts without a few pats on the back."

The sheriff grinned. "We're lucky to have you."

"So, you're telling me I have to lay off work for a few days?" Rachel asked, getting back to the subject.

Sheriff Faulkner nodded. "Based on the doc's recommendation, you need to give your head a rest."

"That's bullshit," Rachel grumbled. "I'm fine. Just a little banged up from the tumble."

"And how do you plan on getting to work?" the sheriff asked. "Seems your SUV is upside down in a ditch."

Rachel sighed. "Okay. I get it. I need to take care of business before I report back to work."

The sheriff nodded. "That's right. But when you do come back, don't expect any special treatment."

Rachel snorted. "Like you would give it."

The sheriff held out his hand to Griff. "Thanks again for taking care of my deputy. I'll call a wrecker to get your vehicle out of the ditch. You're lucky you landed in a ditch and not at the bottom of a cliff."

"I know," Rachel said. "I'd still like to get my hands on the guy who ran me off the road."

"You and me both," the sheriff said. "I'll ask around."

She shook her head. "With so many ATVs in the area, good luck narrowing it down."

The sheriff pushed through the swinging door as the orderly arrived. "We're taking you for a ride to your four-star suite on the second floor."

"Oh good," Rachel said. "If they have room service, I want a pepperoni pizza and a beer."

"Ha," the order said. "The best you'll get is to order from our local pizza restaurant. They deliver here."

"Good to know." Rachel grinned and cocked an eyebrow toward Griff.

"On it." Griff pulled his cell phone out of his pocket as he followed Rachel down the hallway and into the elevator.

By the time they reached her room, Griff had

ordered pizza. "Sorry," he said. "They don't deliver beer."

A nurse entered the room smiling. "I can't get you a beer, but we have sodas and an ice machine. The doctor doesn't have you on any dietary restrictions. All you have to do is name your poison and share a slice of your pizza." She winked.

Rachel laughed and winced. "Hold the jokes until the pain meds kick in."

"Gotcha. I'm Angela. I'll be your nurse through the night. I'll be checking on you regularly to make certain you don't have any issues with the concussion."

"Translated to mean you'll be waking me every fifteen minutes to make sure I'm still alive?" Rachel sighed.

"Maybe not every fifteen minutes." Angela smiled. "But you get the idea."

"I'll be here as well," Griff said.

"We don't usually allow visitors past nine o'clock," Angela said.

"I'm not a visitor," Griff said. "I'm her... fiancé." He met Rachel's gaze and gave an almost imperceptible wink.

Rachel nodded. "That's right. He's my fiancé."

"In that case," the nurse said, "he's family. You're allowed one family member to stay the night with you." She nodded toward the chair beside the bed.

"That chair lies almost flat. I'll bring an extra pillow and blanket."

"Thank you," Griff said.

As the nurse left the room, she almost ran into the two men standing outside the door. "Oh," she exclaimed. "Here to see Ms. West?"

The taller man with black hair and brown eyes said, "We are."

The nurse held the door for them. "Visiting hours end at nine o'clock."

The slightly shorter man smiled. "Thank you, ma'am."

The two men entered the room and let the door swing shut.

Griff crossed the room and held out his hand. "Cog, good to see you."

"Same." The taller man grabbed his hand and pulled him into a hug. When he stepped back, his brow dipped. "Sorry to hear about the team."

Griff's mouth tightened into a thin line. "Yeah. Me, too."

"But we're glad you decided to join us." Cog turned to the man beside him. "You remember Hank Patterson?"

Griff's lips curled upward on the corners. "I remember you as 'Montana.'" He held out his hand.

Hank took it and grinned. "I go by Hank these days. Since I live in Montana, it makes more sense. Less confusing." He gave Griff a hearty handshake and turned toward Rachel. "Who's your friend?"

Griff left the two men to stand beside Rachel's hospital bed. "This is Rachel West. Rachel, meet Jake Cogburn and Hank Patterson. Both men are Navy SEALs, now leading the efforts of the Brotherhood Protectors."

Jake tipped his head toward Hank. "Hank's the founder of the group. Like he said, he lives in Montana where he started the Brotherhood."

Hank nodded. "And Jake runs the Colorado division. Griff tells us you were run off the road on your way out to the ranch."

Rachel's lips twisted. "That's right. Thus, the night I get to spend here."

Jake frowned. "I've seen you around town. Aren't you the new sheriff's deputy?"

"Not so new. I've been here for three months. But yes," she said. "Actually, I was on my way out to see you. I was running into JoJo at the coffee shop so often that we've become friends." Rachel smiled. "I told her about some of the troubles I've encountered since I came to Fool's Gold. She suggested I talk with you and see if the Brotherhood Protectors can help."

Jake nodded. "JoJo's special. Don't know what we'd do without her ability to keep anything mechanical running." His brow furrowed. "What troubles are you encountering?"

Rachel glanced around at the three men, feeling a

little foolish under their scrutiny. "It could all be in my head. I could be too sensitive or downright paranoid, but I think I'm being watched."

Griff reached for her hand. "Any incidents in particular that make you feel that way?"

She nodded and stared up into his eyes. "For my past three night shifts, I've had someone fall in behind my vehicle and follow me for several blocks. When I slowed, he slowed. If I turned a corner, he turned the corner, always staying back far enough I couldn't get the make and model of the car."

Hank frowned. "But it was a car?"

She nodded. "When I executed a U-turn, he turned down another street. I tried to follow, but it was as if he'd completely disappeared."

"Three nights?" Jake asked.

She shrugged. "That I was aware of. He could've been following me before, but I might not have recognized it as being stalked. And I live in an apartment on the second floor. My living room window looks out over the parking lot. I swear I've seen a man standing in the shadows on the other side of the parking lot, facing my window on more than one night."

"Doesn't sound like anyone's committing any crimes," Jake said. "There's no law dictating how you spend your time, as long as you're not trespassing or harming others."

"Yeah, I know," Rachel shoved her hair back from

her face. "That's why I haven't said anything to the sheriff. I don't want to appear paranoid. But here's the kicker..." She looked around at the three men hoping they would understand. "I came to Fool's Gold because of a murder committed here. I'm working at the Sheriff's department, partly because I need a job but also so that I have access to the case files and the authority to investigate cases. You see, the case I'm interested in hasn't been solved. The murderer left only one clue, a wedding veil around the victim's throat. He strangled her on a hiking trail west of here."

"Who was she?" Jake asked.

Rachel swallowed hard past the lump in her throat. "Lindsay Stratton...my sister."

Griff's hand tightened around hers. "You moved here to avenge your sister?"

She nodded and then shook her head. "Yes and no. Yes, he shouldn't be allowed to get away with murder. No. He's still out there. He could do it again. I don't want what happened to my sister to happen to another woman."

"Do you think the person following you might be the killer?" Hank asked.

"I don't know. He hasn't made a move to come out in the open." She snorted. "Hell, I could be imagining it all."

"You're a cop," Hank said. "Have you relied on your instincts before?"

She nodded. "And my gut usually has it right."

"Then you're doing the right thing by contacting us," Jake said. "At the very least, we can provide you protection against whoever is stalking you."

"And we might be able to help you in your search for the killer," Hank said. "My computer guy is good at sifting through data. I can have him take a look."

"I have access to criminal and crime databases," Rachel said. "I've looked for similar cases in this area and in the state over the past five years. Nothing's come up. I've talked with Lindsay's fiancé. He was as shaken as I was."

"Did he have an alibi?" Griff asked.

Rachel nodded. "He was supposed to go on that hike that day, but he couldn't because one of the guys at the store where he works had car trouble and couldn't make it in. He was the only one who could. His supervisor vouched for him, the time clock showed he clocked in and video footage at the store showed him there at the time of the murder." She shook her head. "It wasn't him."

"Where did Lindsay work?" Jake asked.

"At the Coffee Shack on Main Street. She was a barista," Rachel said. "She'd go in early and get off early, which was perfect for her, and usually, for her fiancé. They had the afternoons to enjoy the mountains. In the winter, they'd ski, in the summer, they always had a hike planned."

"They questioned the staff at the coffee shop?" Griff asked.

Rachel nodded. "The sheriff and the state police questioned half the town. No one saw anything that made them think my sister was being stalked. No one approached her that they knew of. She was happy with her fiancé and loving life." Rachel looked down at her hands. "Until someone took that from her." She looked up again. "Lindsay was my family. We were half-sisters, but I didn't love her halfway. I loved her with my whole heart."

"I'm sorry for your loss," Griff said. "Words don't mean much, but I promise to help you in any way I can."

Jake and Hank grinned.

"Congratulations, Griff." Hank stepped forward, holding out his hand. "You've just found your first assignment as a Brotherhood Protector."

Griff frowned. "I don't know what you mean. I haven't interviewed, and I would do this for Rachel with or without being an employee of your team."

"We like to think of our members as teammates, not employees," Jake said. "We work together."

"I don't make much money as a sheriff's deputy," Rachel said.

Hank shook his head. "Money isn't why we do this. My wife was my first 'assignment.' When she was in trouble, she needed someone to protect her. I filled that role, and we made it through." He grinned.

"We've been married for several years and have two beautiful kids."

Rachel frowned. "Are you saying I'm going to end up married with kids after this 'assignment'?" She chuckled. "That's not quite what I had in mind. I need someone to have my back until I know if the threat is real or my imagination."

Hank grinned. "My point is that Sadie and I understand the importance of protecting those who can't always protect themselves."

Jake picked up from there. "Like you said, Rachel, you need someone who has your back. The men of the Brotherhood Protectors are highly trained in special operations. They understand what it means to have your six, and they have the weapons and hand-to-hand combat training that can keep you alive."

Hank nodded. "Sadie and I don't require all of our clients to pay for those services. If they don't have the means to pay, we help anyway. It's our way of giving back. We don't want anyone to suffer because they can't afford to hire the help they need. We're blessed that we can afford to pay our guys no matter how, or if, we get paid for the services they provide."

Rachel nodded. "Thank you. Hopefully, it's all in my head, and it won't take too much of your time to figure it out."

"We'll stay with you until we know for certain," Jake said. He tipped his head toward Griff. "Or rather, Griff will be with you if he chooses to accept this mission."

"I told you, I'd do this with or without the Brotherhood. You don't have to pay me for this job."

"We want you to work with us," Jake said. "*I* want you to work with us. I know your skills and what you'd bring to our organization."

"I'm not the same man I was six months ago," Griff said through gritted teeth.

Rachel studied the man. He was right. His face was leaner, dark circles created shadows beneath his eyes and he had a haunted, sad look that pulled at her heart.

"None of us are the men we were when we were on active duty." Jake bent and pulled up his pants leg, exposing a prosthetic leg attached at the knee. "I didn't think I had anything left to offer when I lost my leg." He gave a crooked grin. "I was wrong. Physicality isn't the only requirement of this job. What we learned up here," he tapped his head, "is even more important."

Hank nodded. "It took a while to convince Jake he had huge potential. Tell you what… Let this assignment be a test. We can see if you have what it takes, and you can see if this is what you want."

Griff's frown deepened as his gaze fixed on Jake's leg, now covered by denim. "I didn't know."

"It doesn't matter," Jake said. "If anything, it makes

me a better man. I've learned not to take myself so seriously and to capitalize on what I have."

Griff stared from Jake to Hank and back to Jake. "Okay. I'm in. But I won't take pay for helping Rachel. And she's not an assignment."

Jake cocked an eyebrow. "Mission, then?"

Griff's frown grew even fiercer. "No. My last mission was a complete failure. I lost every man on my team." His hand, still holding Rachel's, tightened.

Rachel's finger hurt in his grip, but she wouldn't say anything. The man was hurting more inside than the pain he was causing her hand. No wonder he hadn't been in contact with her.

"Are you sure you want me on your team?" He shook his head. "My track record ended in flames." He looked down at Rachel. "And that goes for you, too. Do you want a washed-up SEAL covering your six?"

"If Griff doesn't do the job, we'll assign another one of our team to provide the protection you need," Jake assured Rachel.

"No," Griff said. "I'll do the job."

Jake lifted his chin toward Rachel. "She might prefer someone else."

She shook her head. "I prefer Griff."

Jake grinned and pounded Griff on the back. "Welcome to the Brotherhood Protectors. Your probationary period begins now."

CHAPTER 4

GRIFF STAGGERED under the force of Jake pounding on his back. His shoulder ached. He wasn't quite sure what he'd agreed to, but he knew he couldn't trust anyone else to safeguard Rachel West. Knowing she was investigating a murder was bad enough.

If she was being followed, it could be the murderer.

Griff couldn't walk away from Rachel now. She was alone, had no family to look out for her and was vulnerable. Yes, she was a law enforcement officer and knew how to handle a gun.

Every Navy SEAL knew how to handle weapons and defend himself. What they'd learned in BUD/S and throughout their deployments was that they weren't alone. They had each other's backs. Teamwork had been key to their survival on most missions.

And not getting shot out of the sky by an ISIS rebel with an RPG.

Jake clapped his hands together. "Now that that's settled, do you have a place to stay?"

Griff glanced at Rachel. "No. I just got to town."

"You can stay at the Lost Valley Lodge," Jake said. "We keep several rooms available for when we have new guys transitioning into the area."

"I have a two-bedroom apartment," Rachel said. "You could have the spare bedroom until you can secure a place of your own. You'll need to get a bed, though. I only furnished one of the rooms. I wanted a one-bedroom, but they only had a two-bedroom available when I was looking for a place to live. I do have a couch you can sleep on tonight."

"I've slept on worse," Griff said. "If I'm to have your back, I need to be close." He turned to Jake. "I'll stay with Rachel."

Jake nodded. "I can have a bed brought over tomorrow. For now, we'll leave you two."

"I'm headed back to Montana tomorrow," Hank said. "I'll get Swede digging into the internet and criminal databases to see if he can come up with any similar cases."

Rachel nodded. "Thank you. Though I'll be on leave for a few days, I don't plan on watching TV and eating bonbons. I'll be at the sheriff's office going through the criminal databases again. There has to be something. This guy can't be a one-and-done killer. The wedding veil was his signature…a statement."

Hank pulled out his wallet and extracted a business card. "Let Jake know if you find anything. If you can't get Jake, call me. We're here for you."

She smiled. "Thank you."

As Jake and Hank left the room, Griff followed them to the door. He glanced back. "I'm just stepping outside. I'll be right back."

She smiled. "I'm not going anywhere."

Griff let the door swing shut behind him.

Hank and Jake were waiting for him.

"You'll need to come out to the Lodge tomorrow and get familiar with our office and what we have available to our team," Jake said. "You might find things that will make your job easier, like weapons, communications and tracking devices."

Griff nodded. "I'll bring Rachel."

"Good. It wouldn't hurt for her to know what's available as well," Jake said.

"She's smart and capable, based on her experience with the California Highway Patrol and now the sheriff's department," Hank said. "She had the good sense to know when she needed backup."

Griff's lips lifted on the corners. "And she doesn't take shit from anyone. I saw her twist another Navy SEAL's arm behind his back when he dared to smack her ass as she passed him at McP's. It embarrassed him more than anything. She could have hurt him, but she didn't."

Jake grinned. "The asshole deserved it."

"It happened so fast I didn't have time to throw a punch." Griff shook his head. That was about the time he'd realized he was falling for her.

Rachel was the kind of woman who could take care of herself. A Navy SEAL who was subject to being called up at any moment couldn't maintain a relationship with a woman who couldn't take care of herself. He'd be a fool to try. Rachel was perfect. Tough, beautiful and independent. He'd looked forward to getting to know her better and had envisioned a future with her.

Then deployment. The crash. And...things had changed.

"We'll see you tomorrow at the lodge," Jake said.

"Again, welcome aboard." Hank shook Griff's hand once more. "We need good men like you."

Hank and Jake walked to the elevator. When the doors opened, a man carrying a pizza box stepped out.

Griff dug his wallet out of his pocket, extracted some bills and met the delivery guy halfway down the hall.

"Are you John Griffin?" the young man asked.

Griff nodded. "I am."

"This is your pie."

Griff took the box and handed the guy the bills. "Thank you."

He turned to find Nurse Angela carrying two cups full of ice, with two cans of soda in her pockets. "Perfect timing," she said.

Griff let her enter Rachel's room first, following her in with the pizza.

Rachel grinned. "Thank goodness. I'm so hungry I could eat that entire pizza by myself."

"It's a good thing I ordered a large one," Griff said.

The nurse set the cups of ice onto a table and rolled it over to Rachel. She pulled the cans out of her pockets and laid them on the table. "I'll leave you to your meal. If you need anything, press the button."

"Aren't you staying for a slice?" Rachel asked.

Angela shook her head. "I've already had dinner but thank you for offering. I see you at the coffee shop sometimes. Thank you for your service to this community."

Rachel's cheeks flushed pink. "You're doing more good for the people of this community than I could ever hope to do."

"You're sweet," Angela said and turned to Griff. "And your fiancé is hot. Military?"

He nodded.

"Thank you for your service." She turned back to Rachel, a frown denting her brow. "I swear you remind me of someone."

Rachel stiffened.

The nurse's eyes narrowed, and she touched a finger to her chin. "I think that every time I see you at the coffee shop." Her eyes widened. "There used to be a barista who worked there. You two look so much alike."

Rachel's eyes filled, and her lips thinned.

Angela bit down on her bottom lip. "Such a horrible thing that happened to her. And they still haven't found who did it." She tilted her head. "You know about her?"

Rachel nodded.

"None of the women I know will hike alone anymore. I hope they find him soon. It's scary leaving the hospital in the dark."

"I'll bet," Griff said, ready for the kind nurse to leave.

"Look at me gossiping and such a depressing topic." She shook her head. "I'm going so you can eat before your pizza gets colder." Angela left the room.

Rachel sat silently for a long moment, staring at the door. "I should be used to this by now. I've had more than one person stop me and say how much I looked like the barista at the coffee shop."

"Is that where your sister worked?" Griff asked as he grabbed paper towels from near the sink and spread them across the rolling table in front of Rachel.

She nodded. "I go in there every day for coffee, kind of as a way to capture a view of her life. She'd called me a few days earlier from the coffee shop to say her boyfriend had popped the question, and she'd said yes. Lindsay was so excited about starting the next phase of her life with her Bryan. She was gushing to everyone in the coffee shop." Rachel's mouth turned up in a smile.

"It makes you wonder…" Griff started.

"If the killer was one of her customers?" Rachel nodded. "I had the same thought. She was happy about her engagement and upcoming wedding."

Griff's lips twisted. "Wedding veil."

Rachel nodded. "I go in every day before or after work to people watch. On my days off, I spend most of the day there. It's all I have so far."

"It's a start. And if he's still in the area, he might get cocky and think he's gotten away with—"

"Murder," Rachel whispered. "I keep trying different search criteria against the crime databases. There are so many strangulation cases. I've read through so many of them, but none of the murderers used a wedding veil."

"How far back are you going?" Griff asked.

"I started at two years and then expanded to five. It's taking me so much time to wade through the details. I never would've thought there would be so many strangulations in Colorado alone. My sister is just one more number to add to the statistics of cold cases. I've been going in on my days off to use the computers. The sheriff's department is short-staffed. I have to patrol when I'm on shift."

"Maybe with Hank's guy Swede's help, you can get through more cases faster," Griff suggested.

"I don't know how if Swede isn't in law enforcement."

Griff's lips twisted into a wry grin. "From what I understand, Swede doesn't always go through legal channels to get to the information."

Rachel covered her ears. "I didn't hear that. You realize I'm a member of law enforcement, don't you?"

He chuckled. "Right. You didn't hear that from me. Then again, you want to find your sister's killer, don't you?"

Her lips pursed, and her eyes narrowed. "Yeah, I do."

Griff lifted a shoulder and let it fall. "Just saying, two sets of eyes on the databases beat one."

"True," she said. "I don't know Swede, and I can truthfully say I didn't see him commit any crimes."

Griff grinned. "Especially since he's in Montana, and you're here in Colorado." He selected a slice of pizza, laid it on a napkin in front of Rachel, and then took one out for himself, his stomach rumbling.

"Hungry?" she asked. "When was your last meal?"

He shrugged. "Coffee for breakfast this morning around five o'clock."

"That's it?" Rachel frowned and pushed her slice

of pizza toward him. "Here, you need this more than I do."

"There's enough for both of us and Nurse Angela." He slid the napkin with the pizza on it back toward Rachel. "Eat. You need to keep up your strength. We have work to do on your days off."

She took the slice and sniffed it. "You can't beat pepperoni. I don't understand people who eat cheese pizza. It's like drinking non-alcoholic beer. What's the point?"

Rachel ate two slices. Griff ate four, making up for missed meals that day.

Griff carried the box with the last two slices of pizza to the nurses' station and offered them to the nurses manning the night shift.

Angela laughed. "Are you sure you've had enough?"

Griff nodded and patted his flat belly. "Absolutely. If you don't eat it, I'll just have to throw it away."

"Well, we can't waste good pizza," Angela said. "Thank you."

Griff turned away.

"Sir," Angela said behind him.

He faced her with one eyebrow cocked. "Yes?"

"I didn't mean to upset Ms. West. It's just that the resemblance was so strong, it's positively spooky."

Griff didn't share with the nurse that Lindsay, the barista, had been Rachel's half-sister. Rachel hadn't mentioned it. The sisters had different last names.

There was no reason for anyone to think they'd been sisters other than by their looks. Rachel might be better off keeping her relationship with her sister to herself. Then again, the killer had proven himself smart enough to leave no traceable evidence. If he was following Rachel, he might have figured out the family connection.

"Hey, while you're here…" Angela jumped up, ran to a cabinet and returned with a pillow and a blanket. "It can get really cold in here at night.

Griff thanked her and took the blanket and pillow from her arms. He returned to Rachel's room to find her lying back against the pillow, her eyes closed.

"I'm not asleep," she murmured.

"Yet," he added.

"True." She cracked open an eyelid. "I see you're all set to camp out with me." Her brow puckered. "You probably don't have to stay the night here. The nurses will keep an eye on me to ensure I don't die of a brain bleed."

Griff dropped the blanket on the end of her bed, sat in the lounge chair beside her and tucked the pillow behind his head. "I'm staying."

She turned on her side and tucked her hand beneath her cheek. "I could give you the key to my apartment, and you could sleep in my bed tonight. After being on the road for so long, I'm sure you need a good night's sleep."

"I might get a good night's sleep if someone

wouldn't insist on talking." He cocked an eyebrow in challenge.

She clapped her other hand over her mouth. "Sorry." The silence lasted a couple of moments. "One more thing and I promise to be quiet."

He gave an exaggerated sigh. "Go ahead."

"I'm glad it was you who found me in that ditch," she said softly. "Thank you for saving my life."

"You'd have gotten out."

She shook her head. "I could've been in that ditch a long time before anyone found me. It gets cold in the mountains at night. I could've died of smoke inhalation. I was struggling to breathe, the seatbelt was that tight, and the vehicle could've burst into flames. You saved me from all those possibilities. Not to mention, if the ATV driver was the killer, he could've come back to finish what he'd started."

Griff's heart clenched. "I'm glad I was there," he said. "I never thought I'd run into you here in Colorado." Or back in San Diego after he'd refused to contact her over the last six months. He'd thought he'd completely lost track of her and had secretly mourned the loss.

Rachel reached out and took his hand in hers. As promised, she didn't say anything else. Soon, her hand grew slack, and her breathing deepened. She was asleep.

Griff studied her face, committing every curve, line and flutter of her dark lashes to memory. This was the face he'd dreamed about while in Syria. Hers was the image engraved in his mind that had gotten him through physical therapy when it had hurt so much that he'd wanted to quit. Though he hadn't contacted her, he'd wanted to. He just couldn't weigh her down with his baggage.

Knowing she'd endured the trauma of her sister's murder alone made Griff sick. He'd been feeling sorry for himself while she'd had to arrange for a funeral with no other family members to support her in her grief.

Yes, she could do a lot better than a broken SEAL who had spent so much time wallowing in his own self-pity.

He looked down at her hand in his. Though smaller, it was strong and capable. Like Rachel.

Griff vowed to himself that he'd protect her with his life and help her find her sister's killer. Then he'd get the hell out of her life and let her find someone more worthy of her affection.

He lifted her hand to his lips and pressed a feather-light kiss to the backs of her knuckles.

"I missed you," she whispered so softly he thought he'd imagined the words.

He settled back in the lounge chair, still holding her hand, reflecting on what had just occurred that evening. How had fate led them to the same place, the same day and time? And they'd both lost people they'd loved—family, if not by blood, then by what was in their hearts.

When he was sure she was sound asleep, he whispered, "I missed you, too."

Tasked with keeping her safe, he prayed he was successful in this mission. Failure was not an option.

CHAPTER 5

Rachel woke to sunlight streaming through the window, warming her face. She blinked her eyes open and closed them again.

Raising her hand to shield her face from the glare, she dared to open her eyes again.

Her first thought was of Griff. She turned toward his chair.

Her heart sank. The chair was empty.

The door swung open, and a nurse entered. "Good morning, Ms. West. I'm Jenny. I'm here to get you ready for discharge. As soon as the doctor makes his rounds, we fully expect he'll let you go home."

"Great," Rachel said and pushed to a sitting position.

Nurse Jenny ran Rachel's vitals and charted her results. "Everything appears normal. The doctor should be here shortly." The nurse started for the door. "If you need anything, just press the button."

Rachel needed to know where Griff had gone. He'd been in the chair all night. She knew because she'd woken up every hour, startled out of her sleep by the nightmare of her tumbling over a cliff in her SUV.

Griff had squeezed her hand each time and spoken quiet words of encouragement.

Rachel had fallen asleep each time, relieved to know he'd been there the entire time.

Until now.

Jenny had her hand on the door when Rachel stopped her with, "Could I get a hairbrush and a toothbrush?"

Jenny smiled over her shoulder. "Absolutely. I'll be right back." True to her word, she was gone no more than a minute and was back with a cheap, plastic hairbrush, a toothbrush wrapped in plastic and a small tube of toothpaste.

"Thank you," Rachel said, happier about the generic toiletries than seemed possible.

When Jenny left the room and the door closed behind her, Rachel flung back the sheet and slowly swung her legs over the side of the bed. Because she was alone, she didn't want to risk a fall, unsure of her stability after the head injury.

Rachel eased her feet to the floor, held onto the bed and straightened.

No dizziness, weakness of the knees or blurred vision. She felt practically normal, except she needed a shower and clean clothing. She couldn't walk out of the hospital in the open-back gown. What she'd worn into the hospital was covered in dirt and smelled of smoke. However, they would have to do until she could get home, take a shower and find something clean to wear.

Rachel grabbed her clothes, which were inside a plastic bag on a shelf, ducked into the bathroom to change, washed her face and brushed her teeth. Her hair took a little longer to work through all the tangles and clumps of dried blood. It needed to be cleaned, but that would have to wait.

When every tangle had been smoothed, she sighed at her wan complexion and the goose-egg knot on her forehead.

"Take me as I am," she said to her reflection, then turned and left the bathroom.

Her heart leaped.

Griff stood near the bed, a cup of coffee in each hand. "Oh, good. You're up. I thought you might want some caffeine."

"You really are a life-saver." She grinned as she took one of the cups.

"I have creamer and sugar in my pocket," he offered.

She shook her head. "I like my coffee strong and

black." She tipped the cup up, took a tentative sip and nearly gagged.

Her face must have shown her reaction.

Griff chuckled. "Not good?"

She lifted her chin. "You try it and tell me."

"I've had many different variations of coffee throughout my life. How bad can this be?" He took a sip from his cup, maintaining a straight face throughout. When he lowered the cup, he grinned.

"You're kidding, right?" Rachel stared harder, looking for a chink in his set face. "You can't love that coffee. I can't be with a man who would drink that swill and dare call it coffee."

He blinked twice, and his face screwed up in disgust. "You're right; that's not coffee." He took her cup from her hand, carried both to the sink, dumped the contents and tossed the cups in the trash. After rinsing the sink, he returned to Rachel.

She chuckled. "Thanks for trying. When I get clearance to leave, we'll go get a *real* cup of coffee."

"Sounds good." He scrubbed his hand over the stubble on his chin. "I could use a shower and a shave before we do that."

Rachel smiled and looked down at her dirty jeans and torn shirt. "I need one, too. We could stop by my apartment before we go to the coffee shop. I have coffee there, but that's about all. I haven't been grocery shopping for a while."

"We can accomplish a lot after a shower," he said.

"Agreed." Rachel tamped down the butterflies beating against the inside of her stomach at the thought of Griff naked in her shower. She was a job to him, not her boyfriend and certainly not her fiancé.

"Since I'll be tagging along with you, and we've already established our relationship with the hospital staff, what do you think about continuing to tell folks we're engaged? It might help keep any questions at bay."

Her stomach turned a somersault. "Okay. It's easier to stick to one story than to have to remember who we've said what to."

He nodded. "How do you feel this morning?"

She smiled. "Better than I expected. Some bruising, but nothing I can't handle. I'm ready to get to work and use my time off to really dig into this case. Something has to surface. I refuse to give up."

"And if the killer's your stalker," Griff said, "the sooner we find him, the better."

Rachel nodded. "We must find him before he makes another move." She smiled. "I'm glad you'll be with me. I'm confident in my ability to take care of myself, but I can't always be looking behind me."

"That's where I come in," Griff said.

The door opened, and the doctor entered. "Ms. West, the night shift nurses don't want you to leave." His brow wrinkled. "Something about sharing pizza?" He nodded toward the bed. "If you could take a seat, I'll check you out and sign your discharge papers. I don't have a medical code for sharing pizza that would keep you here longer when you're perfectly fine." He winked.

Rachel perched on the edge of the bed.

The doctor shined a light into each eye and asked a few questions, and then the exam was over. "Try to keep the wheels on the ground from now on. We can't afford to lose our law enforcement officers." As he left, the nurse came in with her discharge instructions and went over what she should do and when to seek medical attention should her condition change.

A few short minutes later, Rachel and Griff opted to take the stairs to the first floor and left the small hospital.

She sighed. "I guess we have to stick together. I'm down a vehicle."

"And I have one." Griff held the passenger door for her. "But if you feel the need to drive, just ask. I'm not holding you accountable for flipping your vehicle. You did good not to hit the guy on the ATV when he deserved it."

"Thank you for offering." She climbed up into the passenger seat and buckled her seatbelt securely. "After last night's crash landing, I'm fine with letting you man the steering wheel."

"Deal," he said and got into the driver's seat. "Where to?"

"My apartment is around the corner," Rachel said.

"We could probably have walked, but I figure you don't want to leave your truck sitting in the hospital parking lot."

She directed him down the street to her apartment, the bright blue Colorado sky making her feel hopeful and happier than she'd been in the six months since her last conversation with her sister.

Rachel had survived a crash that could have taken her life. She was riding in a truck with the man who'd saved her from the wreckage. And he was the Navy SEAL she'd been well on her way to falling in love with back in San Diego and thought she'd never see again.

Yeah, life was pretty good at that moment. Her medical leave from patrol duty would give her the time to dig into the data and really focus. And having Griff to bounce ideas off would be an advantage. With Swede up in Montana working the case from a different angle, they had a chance of nailing the bastard.

After Griff parked in the apartment complex's parking lot, Rachel dropped down from her seat before Griff could come around to open her door. She wasn't used to being treated like a lady. She'd spent so many years trying to be "one of the guys" as a police officer and deputy, she wasn't comfortable with the niceties of good old-fashioned chivalry.

Griff grinned as he pulled a duffel bag out of the back seat and slung it over his shoulder.

Rachel could swear he could read her mind. Heat spread up her neck into her cheeks. She hoped he couldn't. If he knew she'd pictured him naked in her shower, she'd curl up and die of embarrassment. The tough she-cop lusting after the Navy SEAL, who was now her bodyguard, seemed silly, even to her.

But there she was, breathing hard going up the stairs to her apartment. Her breathing had nothing to do with what kind of shape she was in and everything to do with what kind of shape was underneath Griff's jeans and T-shirt.

At the top of the stairs, she stopped short. "Damn."

"What?"

"Keys." She shook her head. "The key to my apartment is on the keyring in my SUV."

"Can we get a spare key from the apartment manager?" Griff asked.

"Maybe," Rachel said. "If she's in."

Griff dropped his duffel bag beside her door and followed her down the stairs and to the office at the opposite end of the building.

Fortunately, Sharon Morgan, a forty-seven-year-old divorcee, was there dressed to the nines in cream slacks with a matching jacket and a black cashmere top. Her bleached-blond hair hung straight to her shoulders, her makeup was perfect, and she wore a ready smile to greet anyone who walked through the door.

"Ms. West, so good of you to stop in. What can I do for you?"

"I've lost my key to my apartment, and my spare is inside the apartment. Could I get you to loan me a key or unlock the door?"

Sharon rose gracefully from her desk chair. "Yes, of course." She unlocked a box on the wall and grabbed a ring of keys. "I'll unlock the door for you. And I can have another spare made for you."

"Thank you," Rachel said.

"And who is this handsome man with you?" Sharon asked, looking up through her beautifully long, false eyelashes.

"This is Griff, my…fiancé." She turned to Griff. "Griff, this is Sharon, our apartment manager."

Sharon held out a perfectly manicured hand, placing the tips of her fingers in Griff's palm. "Pleasure to meet you." She smiled up at him and batted her eyes.

Rachel wished she could dress the way Sharon did and wear everything with the same confidence. The sad truth was that Sharon was beautifully feminine, and Rachel was more of a perpetual tomboy. She sighed and followed the timeless beauty out of the office and walked alongside her the length of the building and up to her apartment.

Sharon slipped the master key into the lock and pushed open the door. She smiled and stood back. "Looks like you have something on the floor. A gift, maybe?" Sharon winked at Griff. "I love a man who leaves me gifts." She touched Rachel's arm. "He's a keeper. Let me know if you need anything else. I'll be in my office until 2:00 pm."

The office manager left, descending the stairs like a pageant queen, smooth, elegant and completely in control while wearing four-inch heels.

"How does she do that?" Rachel sighed. "I could never look that good."

"You're a natural beauty."

"Which is man-speak for girl-next-door or kid sister." She snorted. "I'm hopeless when it comes to being that well put together." She started to step across the threshold. "What was she saying about a gift?" Then she saw it—a Tiffany blue box with a matching bow.

Rachel frowned. "That's not mine."

Griff stepped around her and inspected the box without picking it up. "Does anyone besides the apartment manager have a copy of your apartment key?"

She shook her head. "No. Or at least, not that I know of. Don't touch it. There might be prints."

When she started forward, Griff grabbed her arm. "Let me clear the apartment." Griff slipped his handgun from his holster, held it in front of him and then moved from the entrance into the first room on the right. He emerged a few seconds later and entered the guest bathroom. One by one, he searched each room quickly and efficiently.

When he came out of her bedroom, he placed his handgun back in the holster beneath his jacket.

Her instinct was to say that she could have done the same. Instead, she let him do his job. "Thank you." Rachel hurried past the box and into her small kitchen. She reached into the cabinet beneath the sink, pulled a surgical glove out of a box and grabbed a paper lunch bag.

Slipping her hand in the glove, she returned to the front entrance, lifted the box with her gloved hand and dropped it into the paper bag. "We'll take this to the station after we get showered. I don't know who left it there or how he got in, but this is creepy."

Griff stepped outside, grabbed his duffel bag next to the door and stepped back into her apartment. "Which shower do you want me to use?"

She tipped her head toward a room to the right. "That's the guest bedroom. I'll clean it out later so you can get a bed in there. The bathroom is the next door." She stepped up to the apartment's front door and peered out, searching the shadows of the trees on the opposite side of the parking lot. "I saw the shadowy figure among those trees a couple of nights when I got off work at midnight."

Griff stood beside her and nodded. "I'll check it out."

"I waited until the next morning to look for footprints. I didn't find any, but the dirt appeared to have been brushed with something. It was too smooth." She stepped back and closed the door, twisting the deadbolt. "Do you think whoever left the box retrieved my keys from my crashed SUV?"

Griff shrugged. "It's possible."

"Great," Rachel said. "Add having the locks rekeyed to my to-do list. I'm headed for a shower. If you get done before me, help yourself to anything you can find to eat or drink. I'm sorry to say, you probably won't find much. Or we can stop by Mattie's Diner. They serve breakfast all day."

"I'd like to go to the coffee shop where your sister worked sometime today," Griff said.

Rachel nodded. "As weird as it sounds, I feel closer to her there. I could picture her working behind the counter, serving coffee. She always liked the fancy kind."

Griff grinned. "Not you."

"Not me." Rachel gave him a crooked grin. "I'm pretty basic in what I wear and what I eat and drink. Lindsay was more the adventurer, trying new places and new food and drinks."

"Basic is good." Griff touched her cheek. "You don't have to compare yourself to others. You're special just as you are."

"Thank you." Rachel grimaced. "Right now, I'm sure I smell special—like a smoking engine. See you in a few minutes."

Rachel left before she was tempted to lean into Griff's hand and beg him for a kiss.

They'd been on three dates before he'd deployed, and they'd kissed several times, mostly standing in front of her apartment door. They hadn't gotten past kissing.

In the past six months, Rachel wished she'd invited him into her apartment and her bed, thinking that after making love, she'd have known if he was as good in bed as he was at kissing. Her curiosity would have been satisfied, and she wouldn't have been as depressed about never seeing him again.

Standing in front of him a moment ago, Rachel had recalled how good a kisser he was and wished she'd had the guts to ask him to do it again.

On her way through her bedroom, she grabbed fresh undergarments, a forest green ribbed-knit sweater and jeans. Once in the bathroom, she closed the door and locked it. After a brief second, she unlocked it. If the man was even slightly tempted to come in while she was showering, she wouldn't tell him to leave.

Her shower went uninterrupted, much to her disappointment. She quickly dried her body and wrapped her hair in the towel.

She felt like a new woman with a clean body and hair. After she slipped into her clean clothes, she brushed her hair and left it damp. It would dry in soft curls if she didn't bother to straighten it.

Rachel and Lindsay had looked so much alike. Though they'd had different fathers, they'd looked very much like their mother with her dark curly hair and green eyes. Rachel's stepfather had called Rachel, Lindsay and his wife "his girls."

He'd been a good man who'd loved his girls.

Rachel went back through her room, dug out her hiking boots, pulled on socks and then slipped into the boots. They weren't sexy like Sharon's high heels, but she could run in the boots. She'd break something if she attempted to walk in four-inch heels.

She found her spare key in her nightstand, slipped it into her jeans pocket and stepped out of her room.

Griff stood in the living room, looking out across the parking lot. His blond hair was damp and slicked back from his forehead. He wore a black T-shirt, black jeans and his black leather jacket. With his hair slicked back and damp, he looked like a sexy gang member.

He glanced over his shoulder at her. "Do you close the blinds at night?"

Rachel nodded. "I hadn't up until a few weeks ago. Now, I close all the blinds. I don't like the idea of someone watching me all the time."

"Do you recognize the car directly across the parking lot from my truck?"

"I've seen it before. Why?" she asked.

"It wasn't there when we arrived. Now, it is." Griff glanced down at his smartwatch. "Let's drop the gift at the sheriff's office and let them process it for latent prints."

Rachel scooped up the bag containing the blue box and strode to the door. "While they're processing the gift for prints, we can grab a bite at Maddie's Diner."

Griff's stomach rumbled loudly.

Rachel chuckled. "Let's do this."

"Excuse me." Griff stepped in front of her before she could get far. "Let me take point."

She held up her hands. "Sure. Lead the way."

Griff opened the apartment door and stepped outside onto the landing. He studied the same shadows Rachel had found and said, "Wait here."

She wanted to tell him not to be ridiculous, but she let him do his thing and waited just inside her doorway.

Griff descended the steps to the ground and circled the trees and bush. As quickly as he moved through the brush, he probably wasn't finding anything noteworthy.

Not even a week before, Rachel would have wondered if she'd imagined the shadowy figure. Not anymore. Someone had gone into her apartment and left a box on the floor.

Several long moments later, Griff called up to her, "Come on down."

She left her apartment, locked the door with the spare key and tucked the key into her jeans pocket.

Everything appeared to be in order, with no signs of anyone loitering in the bushes.

Griff helped her into his truck then rounded the hood to slip into the driver's seat.

Rachel gave him directions to the sheriff's department and sat back in her seat.

The building was only a couple of blocks away, so it didn't take long to get there, and they parked near the front entrance.

Griff and Rachel entered the sheriff's office, Rachel carrying the gift.

A deputy stood at the reception desk. "Hey, West. Heard about your accident. Glad you're okay."

She smiled at the young man. "Thanks, Dalton. Is the sheriff in?"

"Yes, I am," Sheriff Faulkner's voice boomed through the open door of his office. "Come in."

Rachel led Griff down a hallway and stopped in the doorway to Faulkner's office.

The sheriff frowned. "What the heck are you doing, coming in here when you're on medical leave?"

"I feel fine," Rachel insisted. "At least until I got this." She set the bag on the table. "Someone left me a present. On the floor...in my locked apartment."

"Damn, West. That's one creepy secret admirer." The sheriff looked inside the bag.

"I haven't opened it or touched it," Rachel said. "I'm hoping I can pull some latent prints from it."

"You're off for the next few days," the sheriff reminded her.

"And since I'm not riding patrol, I wanted to check the databases and see if I can make any more progress."

"It's like looking for a needle in a haystack," Faulkner said. "People don't always add all the information concerning a case. Have you expanded your search past the five years?"

"Not yet," Rachel said. "I'll do that today and see if I can get any cases older than five years of strangulations using a veil or with victims of the same hair color and age as my sister. But first, we're going to get some breakfast at Maddie's Diner."

"Best breakfast in town," the sheriff said.

"Would you like to join us?" Rachel asked.

Sheriff Faulkner shook his head. "I've had breakfast; I'll wait for lunch. Thank you, though. I'll get on checking this gift box for prints and have someone go over to your apartment to dust as well."

Rachel smiled at her boss. "Thank you."

She hooked Griff's arm and left the office. "We can walk from here. It's only a block. That will also give us the opportunity to be seen as an engaged couple."

Griff took her hand in his and stepped out onto the sidewalk. They walked the block in silence and entered Maddie's Diner.

Since it was just past the regular breakfast hours

and too early for lunch, there weren't many people in the diner.

"Seat yourself," the waitress said. "I'll be by in a minute to get your order."

Griff chose a booth in the corner. He settled into the seat with his back to the wall.

"Scoot," Rachel said.

Griff moved over.

Rachel sat beside him. "There. Isn't this cozy, sweetheart?"

He grinned. "Yes, it is, honey."

The waitress returned with a smile. "Hi, Rachel. Who have you got with you today?"

"Candy, this is my fiancé, Griff." She smiled up at Griff. "Griff, this is Candy. Though we've only known each other a few weeks, we're on a first-name basis because, sadly, I eat most of my meals here."

"She does," Candy said, nodding.

"Maddie, the owner, is such a good cook I can't begin to make anything quite as tasty. And it's no fun cooking for one."

Candy wrinkled her nose. "I eat most of my meals here, too. Maddie is the best cook in the state of Colorado." She smiled at Griff. "So, Rachel, you have a fiancé. Why did I not know this?"

Rachel's cheeks heated. "It's all so new. Griff got in town last night."

"He popped the question last night?" Candy

sighed. "How romantic." Her eyes widened. "Show me the ring."

Her cheeks burning now, Rachel had forgotten that most engagements came with a ring. She opened her mouth but couldn't think of an excuse.

"It didn't fit," Griff said. "We're having it sized."

"I'm so happy for you. I was worried you weren't happy being alone in Fool's Gold. And here you had a boyfriend all along." She sighed again. "Seems so mundane now for me to ask what you'd like to eat. We should be celebrating."

"We *are* celebrating," Rachel said. "We're hungry and came to the best restaurant in the whole state. What better way to celebrate than with food we love?"

"Right?" Candy grinned. "Then what is it you'd like to have?"

Griff and Rachel placed orders for a hearty breakfast with eggs, bacon, hashbrowns and toast.

"And please bring coffee," Rachel added.

After Candy left to fill their orders, Rachel shot a glance toward Griff. "I still want to take you to the coffee shop where my sister worked."

"And I want to go there," he said.

"I keep hoping that by going to the places she frequented that somehow a clue will come to me." Rachel gave him a crooked grin. "My sister was the free spirit who believed in fate, Karma and signs. I was the older child...the grounded one. Do you believe in fate?"

"I didn't. But when my entire team was killed in a helicopter crash, I had to believe I was spared for a reason. It's been the only way I can reconcile my survival with their deaths."

"I'm so sorry," Rachel said. "Maybe you were spared to help find my sister's killer."

"I hope that's the case. It pains me greatly to know a man capable of strangling a woman is still free and could strike again."

"Exactly. And he could be a member of this community, someone everyone trusts." She stared across the room at the few customers eating a late breakfast, and a shiver rippled down her spine. "Everywhere I go, I always wonder if he's sitting in the same room as I am. If he's at the gas station when I'm stopping for fuel. Hell, we could be passing each other in the grocery store."

CHAPTER 6

Griff reached for Rachel's hand. "Do you know the people who are in this room now?"

Rachel shrugged. "Some." She tipped her chin toward a table where two men sat in business suits. "I'm not on a first-name basis with those two men, but they have some kind of management positions at the casino. They meet for breakfast quite often or for coffee at the coffee shop. I've also seen them out at the Watering Hole Tavern after work."

"What about the man sitting with the woman in the far corner?" Griff asked.

"I've seen them once before, but not enough to learn anything about them." Rachel tipped her head toward a nice-looking man with salt and pepper hair, seated at the bar. "That's Alan Smith. He's a package delivery driver. I see him all over town. I think he's got a thing for Candy."

"The woman sitting by herself?" Griff asked.

"Phyllis Miller," Rachel said. "Divorced, happily alone and runs the souvenir shop. She has a late breakfast and opens the shop around eleven."

"You have a good handle on the people of Fool's Gold," Griff said.

"Only a few—the ones I see all the time because of my eating and coffee habits."

Griff didn't like the constant frown marring her pretty face. She hadn't had it when she'd been in San Diego. The loss of her sister and the worry about the killer weighed on her.

Griff hoped that by sticking close to Rachel, he'd find the stalker who might turn out to be the killer. The bastard needed to die.

Candy served their meal and coffee. "Coffee is complimentary in celebration of your engagement," she said with a grin.

"Thank you, Candy," Rachel said.

"Yes, thank you," Griff repeated.

"Have you thought about a date? Or is it too soon?" the waitress asked.

"Too soon," Rachel said.

"But the sooner, the better," Griff said. "I don't want her to get away again. We've spent far too much time apart."

"And I'm not one for a big wedding," Rachel said. "The money would be better spent on—"

"The honeymoon," Griff said with a wink.

He loved the way the color rushed up into her cheeks.

"I was thinking the money would be better spent on a down payment for a house."

He nodded. "That, too. After a honeymoon."

Candy laughed. "You two are too cute and obviously in love. I'm happy for you." She left their table and stepped behind the bar to refill Al's mug. "When are you getting married, Al? Surely, you have a dozen pretty girls wishing you would ask."

Al shook his head. "Not interested," he murmured.

"Really? Who was she?"

He frowned. "Who was who?"

"The woman who broke your heart?" Candy cleared away the man's empty breakfast plate and laid his check beside his coffee mug.

Al tossed a bill on the counter and left.

"I guess Alan isn't that into Candy," Griff observed.

"He doesn't usually have much to say. He just delivers packages and goes about his own business."

A man entered shortly after Alan left. He was dressed in dirty blue jeans and a T-shirt with the feed store logo printed across the chest.

"And him," Griff asked.

"Trent Morris," she answered. "Works at the feed store loading livestock feed and heavy items. He likes the coffee at the coffee shop. Or at least someone at the feed store likes it. He comes in for two cups and leaves without drinking them here. I assume he's taking them back to the store for someone else."

They ate in silence, finishing with a top-off on their cooling coffee.

Candy delivered their check. "If you need any assistance planning the wedding, I'd love to help. I've always wanted to be a wedding planner."

"Thank you. I'll let you know." Rachel slid out of her seat and stood.

Griff paid the bill. With a hand to the small of Rachel's back, Griff guided her to the exit and stepped out first, holding the door for her.

She paused before walking through, one eyebrow cocked.

He gave her a twisted grin. "I know. You can open a door all by yourself. But my mama taught me to treat all women with respect and care."

Her smile spread across her face. "I guess I can't fault your mama."

"And it's only what a fiancé would do for the love of his life," he pointed out.

"I wouldn't know. I've never been engaged."

"Until now," he amended.

"Right." She stepped across the threshold, let the door swing shut behind her and shot a quick glance around. "I don't like lying to people. It goes against what my parents taught me."

"They taught you right. But I'm sure they'd

forgive you in this case," he said as he settled his hand once again at the small of her back. "Where to?"

Rachel looked left then right. "Back to the sheriff's office to see if they lifted any prints and what was in the box. Then I'll spend some time digging into the databases again."

They walked the short distance to the sheriff's office and stepped inside.

Sheriff Faulkner and Deputy Dalton stood around the reception desk, staring down at the blue box covered in dark dust.

"Well, did you get any prints?" Rachel asked.

The sheriff frowned. "Not a single one. Not on the box or the contents."

Griff and Rachel moved forward.

"What was inside?" Rachel asked.

Dalton lifted a silver chain with a heart-shaped pendant. "You have a secret admirer." He handed the necklace to Rachel.

She held up her hands instead of taking it.

"It's okay," the sheriff said. "Like I said, not a single print on the box or its contents."

"He's not stupid," Griff said.

Rachel took the necklace. On the face of the heart were the words, *I LOVE YOU.*

"Turn it over," Dalton said.

As Rachel flipped the heart over, Griff leaned over her shoulder and read the engraving on the back.

UNTIL DEATH DO US PART

Rachel stiffened. "That's not at all creepy, is it?"

"Threatening, if you ask me," the sheriff said.

"And in keeping with a man who would strangle a woman with a wedding veil," Griff added.

Sheriff Faulkner nodded. "My thoughts exactly. By the looks of that necklace, I'd guess you're his next target."

Rachel's lips pressed into a line. "That could be a good thing."

"There isn't anything good about being a killer's next target," her boss said.

"If he makes a move on me, it will bring him out in the open. We can catch him."

"I don't even have enough deputies to pull patrol," the sheriff said. "I can't spare one to provide you protection."

Griff shook his head. "You don't have to. I've got her covered," he said. "I'll be with her twenty-four-seven."

The sheriff's eyes narrowed. "So, is the rumor true?"

Rachel's brow puckered. "What rumor?"

"My deputy is engaged?" Sheriff Faulkner frowned and looked from Rachel to Griff and back to Rachel.

Rachel's face flushed bright pink, the color traveling all the way out to her ears.

"Yes, sir," Griff answered for them, sparing Rachel the lying. "She agreed to be my fiancé last night." Which was true, even if only for pretend.

The sheriff's frown deepened. "And you're happy about it?"

Rachel laughed. "Why wouldn't I be? He asked."

"She said yes." Griff slipped his arm around her back.

Rachel slid her arm around him and grinned. "He's stuck with me."

"Please tell me you plan on staying in this area," the sheriff said,

Griff nodded. "I do."

"Good. I can't afford to lose a good deputy."

"I'm not going anywhere," she said.

"And I'll be with her every minute of the day to keep her safe."

"Do you have a gun?" the sheriff asked.

Griff opened his jacket, displaying his shoulder holster and the Glock nestled inside.

Sheriff Faulkner nodded. "Okay then. I'm counting on you to keep her safe."

Griff held up his hand as if swearing-in. "I will."

"Were you able to dust my apartment?" Rachel asked.

"We did," Dalton said. "We found two sets of prints. Yours and another set."

"They could be mine."

Dalton nodded. "If you don't mind, I'd like to get a copy of your prints to compare."

Griff nodded. "Sure."

Dalton brought out a fingerprint card and an ink pad. In less than five minutes, he had Griff's prints scanned in and compared to those they'd lifted in Rachel's apartment.

"They're a match," Dalton said.

The sheriff snorted. "Which means your admirer didn't leave anything for us to go on."

"Did you canvass my neighbors?" Rachel asked. "Did anyone see a man come and go, a strange vehicle?"

Dalton nodded. "Most of your neighbors weren't home."

Rachel's lips pressed together. "They work during the day."

"Right," Dalton said. "Those who were home weren't looking out the windows."

"What about the apartment manager, Ms. Morgan?" Rachel asked.

"She said she didn't get to the building until a few minutes before you came into her office."

"What about the security cameras?" Rachel asked.

Dalton shook his head. "I asked to look at the security footage for the apartment complex. Ms. Morgan said it hasn't been working for the past few days, and she has a firm scheduled to work on it later this week."

Rachel glanced at Griff. "He probably delivered it last night while I was in the hospital."

Griff nodded. "Then it's just as well you weren't home."

"What do you want to do with the necklace?" Dalton asked.

"We should enter it into evidence," the sheriff said.

"If it's okay with you, I'd like to keep it for a while. I promise to admit it into evidence later."

The sheriff's brow furrowed. "Are you sure?"

Rachel nodded. "I want to think about it. I'm trying to get into the killer's head. This could possibly be the only tangible evidence I can get my hands on. The veil has already been admitted as evidence at the state crime lab."

Sheriff Faulkner nodded. "Okay." He turned to Griff. "I'm counting on you to take care of my deputy."

"I'm on it," Griff said.

"Now, if you don't have any objections, I'd like to use the computer to tap into the crime databases," Rachel said. "This guy premeditates. If he's coming after me next, he could've gone after others before my sister. There has to be a connection somewhere."

"I'll leave you to it," the sheriff said. "I have a meeting with the mayor in fifteen minutes."

Rachel led Griff to a room across the hallway from the sheriff's office. She sat in the chair in front of a computer and logged in. Then she glanced up at Griff. "You can grab a spare chair from the sheriff's office. I'm hoping two heads are better than one while looking through these cases. You might see something I'm not considering."

Griff grabbed a chair from Faulkner's office and sat beside Rachel.

"I'm going to expand my search out ten years and see if I get any hits on wedding veils and black-haired females eighteen to forty years old. I didn't find anything specific in my search of cases five years old or less."

For the next few hours, they read through cases of black-haired females who had been strangled. None of them had been strangled with a wedding veil.

Nearing noon Rachel pressed her fingers to her temples.

"Headache?" Griff asked.

She nodded.

"You're pushing too hard."

"I'm fine. I just need something for this headache." She focused on the computer and brought up yet another victim.

"You need to take a break, get some air and rest your eyes."

"Look, if you want to help, read this one for me. I'll close my eyes." She pushed away from the computer and closed her eyes. "I bumped the search out to fifteen years. It's crazy, and I'm insane to keep looking, but I can't give up."

Griff sighed and leaned closer to the monitor. "Christy Severs. Twenty-seven years old, black hair, green eyes, five feet five inches. From Colorado Springs. Disappeared on her way home from her job as a waitress. Cause of death, ligature strangulation. Victim discovered by a janitor in a large waste container behind a warehouse. Victim found with—" Griff's gut clenched.

"With what?" Rachel sat forward.

"A wedding veil over her head," he said softly.

Rachel's face paled. "The case is still open. The perp was never identified."

She scrolled through the data. "Her fiancé was questioned but had an alibi. Her parents put up a reward for any information leading to the arrest of their daughter's killer."

Griff grabbed a pen and paper and scribbled down the names of Christy's parents and the address where they lived. He also wrote down the fiancé's name and address. "It's been fifteen years. What are the chances they live in the same place?"

"I can check them against the Department of Motor Vehicles database." She switched databases. "I'll check Christy's father's name first. If her parents divorced, his name won't have changed." Five addresses popped up when she keyed in Mark Severs and Colorado Springs. One of them was the one from the crime report. The license was current.

Rachel turned to Griff, her face tense. "We're going to Colorado Springs."

"Check for the fiancé," Griff said. "We might get lucky and interview both while we're there."

Rachel scanned for Joseph Penders in Colorado Springs. When she didn't get a hit, she expanded to the entire state. One came up in Denver. "We'll start with Christy's father."

She pushed back her chair and stood.

Griff stood as well.

For a moment, Rachel appeared to be fine. Then her eyes rolled back, she swayed and her knees gave way.

Griff caught her before she hit the ground and hauled her up against him. "Hey," he whispered against her ear. "Talk to me, Rach."

She leaned her head back and blinked. "What...happened?"

He smiled. "You passed out."

Her brow puckered. "I don't pass out."

"Sorry, sweetheart. You just did."

She raised a hand to her head. "I must've gotten up too quickly." Though she was conscious, she didn't try to move away.

Griff was content to hold her for as long as she'd let him. Her body was warm and soft, her breasts pressed against his chest, the scent of her shampoo wrapping around his senses, making him want to bury his hands in her hair and press a kiss to her full, rosy lips. He lowered his head, his mouth so close he could almost taste hers.

She stared up into his eyes for the longest moment.

God, he was tempted.

Hell, he was only human.

Griff brushed his lips across hers, only intending to taste. When she opened to him, he couldn't hold back. He crushed her mouth, his tongue thrusting past her teeth, meeting hers in a primal dance.

How long they remained together, he couldn't be sure. A second...a lifetime...it wasn't long enough.

Somewhere in the back of his consciousness, the sound of footsteps brought him back to his senses. He raised his head.

Rachel's tongue swept across her kiss-swollen lips. "I think I can stand on my own." She pressed her hands against his chest.

Griff loosened his hold around her waist but didn't release her until he was certain she wouldn't fall again.

Rachel straightened. "I'm okay."

He dropped his arms to his sides as the footsteps arrived at the door to the office.

Deputy Dalton stood there. "Just checking to see if you were still here."

"We are, but we're leaving." Rachel pushed past the young deputy.

"Make any headway on your sister's case?" Dalton asked.

"We're not sure." Rachel said. "We're heading to Colorado Springs to find out. I probably won't be back here today."

"I'll let the sheriff know," the deputy said. "Good luck."

Griff hurried to get ahead of Rachel before she left the building, insisting on going first.

"What could possibly happen to me coming out of the sheriff's office?" She shook her head.

"You never know," he said. "Rather safe than sorry."

Rachel allowed him to open her truck door for her, but she refused his hand when he offered to help her up into the truck. As she slipped past him, she was careful not to touch him and climbed unassisted into the passenger seat.

Griff wondered if she was mad at him for kissing her. She couldn't be too mad, not considering how passionately she'd participated.

He closed her door and hurried around to get into the truck.

As he pulled out of the parking lot onto Main Street, a movement out of the corner of his eye made him glance her way in time to see her tongue sweep across her lips.

He didn't say anything until they'd cleared the city limits and were well on their way through Ute Pass, heading toward Colorado Springs.

"Rachel, I'm—" he started.

"Don't," she said sharply.

"Don't what?"

"Don't say you're sorry for what happened back there," she said.

He shook his head. "I wasn't going to. I'm not in the least sorry for kissing you. If anything, I'm sorry it didn't last longer."

She raised her fingers to her lips. "Same." Then she shook her head. "I just can't."

"Can't what?"

She glanced out her side window, turning her face away from him, though her reflection was plain for him to see. "I don't feel right moving on with my life when my sister's was cut short."

Griff understood all too well what Rachel was feeling. Survivor's guilt. He'd lived while others had died. How could he go on when they couldn't? For months, he'd wished he'd died with them. Every breath he took was weighted with the burden of guilt for living when he shouldn't have.

His mental health therapist had helped him process his feelings. But time was what he'd needed and still needed to get past the pressure in his chest when he thought of the brothers he'd lost. Time would help fade the images of that burning helicopter consuming the lives of his friends.

"I can't tell you how to feel," he said. "I've won and lost in the fight with my own demons. What I know in my heart is that every one of my teammates wouldn't have wanted me to give up or put my life on hold because they couldn't live theirs. And I wouldn't have expected them to quit living if I had been the one who'd died in that crash instead of them."

"Lindsay wouldn't have wanted me to put my life on hold. She lived every day of her life to the fullest. She'd want nothing less for me." Rachel drew in a deep breath and let it out slowly. "I just can't move on without closure."

"What if we don't find her killer?" Griff asked.

She shook her head. "That's not an option. I will find him, no matter how long it takes. In the meantime, I need to keep my head in the game."

Griff's lips twitched, but he hid the smile threatening to spread across his face. He liked that he'd shaken her, but he wasn't happy that she was so conflicted about it. "Did our kiss pull you out of the game?"

"Yes." Rachel lifted her chin. "I can't regret it, but we can't do it again. Not until we find Lindsay's killer. He's out there. Watching. If I lose focus, I could die, and he would get away to kill another." Her jaw hardened. "I can't let that happen. I don't want anyone else to go through what I have because of my sister's murderer."

Griff reached across the console for her hand.

She hesitated for a second and then placed her hand in his. "We have to be focused."

He nodded. "Agreed. But for the first time since our helicopter was shot down, I feel alive and that my life is truly worth living." He shot a glance toward Rachel. "You did that. You made me realize that punishing myself wouldn't bring back my brothers. I don't regret that kiss."

CHAPTER 7

RACHEL'S LIPS tingled all the way into Colorado Springs. Kissing Griff had reawakened everything she'd felt when they'd dated back in San Diego. They'd clicked from the moment they'd met in the bar at McP's.

She'd waited anxiously for his calls. When his caller ID flashed across the screen, her heart had pounded, and her breathing grew ragged. The man had her tied in knots in the most delicious way.

In their three dates, he hadn't taken them past heavy petting to consummate their relationship by making love.

She'd thought it sweet at first. But by the end of the third date, her body was a raging forest fire of desire. Then when he hadn't called for a week, she'd wondered if she'd done something to make him back off. Or had he grown bored with her?

Hell, she was a good cop, in great physical shape and good at handling difficult and dangerous situations, but she wasn't good when it came to interacting with men. The badass cop persona she wore every day was necessary for her to fit into her chosen profession and gain the trust and respect of her male colleagues.

Beneath that tough exterior, she was still a woman who wanted to be loved for who she was inside, not who she had to be on the outside.

And she'd thought she'd found a man who wasn't intimidated by her profession, who appreciated her for her, not the woman he thought she should be.

Then her world had crashed with Lindsay's call. When she'd needed him most, he'd disappeared off the face of the earth.

She'd pushed Griff to the back of her mind and focused on justice for Lindsay. The search had helped her through the grief of losing her only relative. And it had helped her through the grief over losing Griff.

She might have been able to function beside him if they'd kept everything on a professional basis, with Griff as the bodyguard and herself as the client. She could have continued to pretend to be an engaged couple. After all, it was playing pretend, and she knew that.

But that kiss.

When he'd claimed her lips, her carefully constructed wall of self-deceit had come tumbling down. It had only been a matter of time before she fell for the man again. Yes, he'd changed. Watching the people he'd cared about go up in flames had left an indelible mark on Griff.

And Rachel had changed as well. Her desire to avenge her sister had become an obsession. Her entire reason for living was to find Lindsay's killer and take the bastard down. She couldn't let a kiss derail her focus. Rachel hadn't been able to stop what had happened to Lindsay. The least she could do was stop it from happening again.

Not a night passed that Rachel didn't slip into nightmares where her sister's scream echoed over and over in her head.

Griff followed the GPS directions taking him to an older subdivision of Colorado Springs. The houses were a mix of well-maintained structures and some that needed fresh paint and the yards mowed.

He parked his truck along the street in front of a white, craftsman-style house with a wide front porch and a royal blue front door.

Rachel's chest tightened. These people had gone through what she'd gone through, losing a young woman who'd meant a lot to them.

Though she hated dragging them back through their pain, they might know something that could help lead them to the killer.

"Ready?" Griff again reached across the console and took her hand, giving it a reassuring squeeze.

Rachel squared her shoulders and nodded. "I am."

She pushed open her door and dropped to the ground, holding onto the truck in case she got weak again.

Her knees held firm.

Griff joined her, and they walked together up the sidewalk and the porch steps, arriving at the front door.

Rachel drew in a deep breath and touched her finger to the doorbell. They waited for a minute, then two. No one answered the door.

"They might be at work," Griff suggested.

"Mark Severs is seventy-one, based on his driver's license birthdate. Hopefully, he's retired." She rang the doorbell again.

A dog barked somewhere behind the house.

When no one answered the second ring, Rachel refused to admit defeat. They had to be home.

She descended the porch steps and turned left rather than walking back to the truck.

"Where are you going?" Griff asked, hurrying to keep up.

"Around back," she said. "They might be in their backyard and can't hear the doorbell."

Griff kept pace, coming to a stop at a wooden gate.

Voices sounded in the backyard. A man's deep one and a woman's muffled response.

"Hello," Rachel called out. "Anyone home?"

The voices stopped.

A few moments later, a man with gray hair opened the gate and peered out. "Can I help you?"

Rachel nodded. "Are you Mark Severs?"

He frowned. "Yes, I am."

Rachel stuck out her hand. "I'm Deputy Rachel West from Fool's Gold in Teller County."

Mr. Severs took her hand. "Ms. West."

"This is my...partner Griff."

Griff took the man's hand. "Nice to meet you."

"What can I do for you?" Mr. Severs asked.

"Sir, do you mind if I ask you some questions about your daughter Christy's case?"

Mr. Severs' lips thinned into a tight line. "It's been fifteen years. Why now?" His eyes narrowed. "Have they come up with anything new?"

"No and yes," Rachel said.

"That should be either a yes or no answer, not both," the man said.

"Could we come in and talk?" Griff asked.

"I don't want you upsetting my wife. She's never gotten over the loss of our only child."

"We'll be brief," Rachel said.

Mr. Severs held the gate wide for them to enter and called out, "Donna, we have company."

A woman with short, salt and pepper hair rose to her feet from where she'd been working in a flower garden. She smiled and brushed the dirt off her hands. "Please, come in."

"They want to ask questions about Christy's case."

Donna Severs' smile faded. "I don't know what good it will do. They never found her killer. That bastard is living free while my only child is buried in a cemetery." She sighed. "But where are my manners? Please, come sit down."

Rachel and Griff crossed the patio to settle into a couple of cushioned outdoor chairs.

"We're very sorry for your loss, Mr. and Mrs. Severs," Griff said.

Rachel nodded. "I can't begin to imagine the pain of losing a child, but I know what it feels like to lose a loved one. I lost my little sister recently."

"Oh, dear." Mrs. Severs' brow furrowed. She reached for Rachel's hands and squeezed them gently. "I'm so very sorry for your loss."

"I'm actually chasing leads in a murder case from six months ago." Rachel swallowed hard on the lump in her throat. "A young woman was strangled while out hiking."

"We heard about that on the news," Mr. Severs said.

His wife shook her head. "A terrible tragedy. Her parents must be beside themselves. We'd give anything to have our Christy back."

Rachel paused, trying to come up with the best way to frame her questions. "I read in your daughter's case file that she was found with a wedding veil over her head."

Mrs. Severs nodded. "It was horrible. So very horrible. What a cruel thing to do. It was like he was mocking her."

"What do you mean?" Rachel asked.

"My Christy's boyfriend had just asked her to marry him the night before. He'd taken her to the Broadmoor for a special dinner. After dinner, he walked her out front of the resort. The trees were all decorated for the coming Christmas season. He asked her to marry him there, and she said yes." Mrs. Severs' eyes filled. "She was so happy. She woke us to show off her ring." The woman pressed a hand to her chest. "Excuse me."

Mrs. Severs jumped up and ran into the house.

"I'm sorry. My wife still gets emotional talking about the last time we saw our daughter alive. She left before we got up the next morning to work a double shift at the Townhouse Restaurant where she worked. She called before she left that evening, excited about looking through the brides' magazines my wife had run out and bought." He looked down at his clasped hands. "You go over and over in your mind what you should have done or said. But it doesn't change the fact that she's gone."

Rachel blinked back tears, her own heart breaking for the Severs and for herself. She'd loved her younger sister with all her heart.

Griff reached for her hand and held it in his.

Mrs. Severs returned to the patio, carrying a large

cardboard box. "This is all we have left of our daughter's things. Her scrapbook from when she back-packed around Europe, her college diploma and the jewelry that made her so happy." The older woman sifted through the box wistfully.

"My daughter taught elementary school." Mr. Severs said. "She worked at the restaurant on the weekends to save money to put down on the purchase of a house. She had built up a nice nest egg."

"Do you mind if I look at her things?" Rachel asked. "I promise to be careful."

"Sure." Mrs. Severs laid the box on the table beside Rachel.

Rachel pulled out the scrapbook and stared down at photos of a girl with black hair and green eyes. Much like her sister. Much like herself.

Mrs. Severs smiled at the photo. "She had the most beautiful ebony black hair." She touched a hand to her short salt and pepper hair. "She got my dark hair and green eyes from her father." She glanced up at Rachel. "Your hair is very much like Christy's was. Black, long and wavy. Such a beautiful girl."

Rachel flipped through more photographs probably taken during high school.

Unsure of what she was looking for, Rachel continued to sift through the cardboard box, setting aside old birthday cards, a stuffed bunny and concert tickets in her attempt to get to the other items buried beneath them. At the bottom, she found a shiny wooden jewelry box.

"Christy bought the box in Spain on her European backpacking adventure." Mr. Severs snorted. "And we were afraid for her the entire time she was gone, never thinking we'd lose her in our own country."

Rachel opened the box and stared down at a pretty array of gold and silver earrings, rings and thin chains. She lifted one of the chains and dropped it back in the box, her hands shaking.

"What's wrong?" Mrs. Severs asked. "You suddenly turned as white as a sheet."

Rachel forced a smile to her lips. "I was involved in an automobile accident yesterday. I'm not quite up to my old self. Thank you for your concern."

"Christy got that necklace the day before Bryan proposed. She was so excited, guessing he would propose soon. When he asked her out to dinner, she wore her nicest dress and the necklace with the sweetest words on it." Christy's mother raised a necklace out of the box and read the inscription. "I love you." She turned the heart over. "Until death do us part." The older woman looked up with tears in her eyes. "She was so excited by his proposal, she forgot to thank him for his other gift."

Rachel glanced toward Griff.

He gave her an almost imperceptible nod, acknowledging the significance of the necklace.

"Did Christy ever mention feeling like she was being watched or followed?" Rachel asked.

Mrs. Severs shook her head. "No, but men were always hitting on her at the restaurant. Some more than others. She managed to keep them at bay. Bryan was the love of her life. My Christy was so beautiful." She stared at Rachel. "She looked so much like you. When I first saw you, I almost believed she'd come back, and her death was just a long and terrible nightmare." Her eyes spilled fresh tears. "I'm sorry. You do look a lot like her." She wiped her cheeks, unable to keep up with the flow of tears.

"Mrs. Severs, do you still keep in contact with Bryan Peterson, Christy's fiancé?"

She nodded. "We send him birthday and Christmas cards every year. He moved to Denver and eventually married a nurse. They have a beautiful little girl. They named her Christy. He brings her to visit when he's in town at his parent's house."

"Do you happen to have his phone number?" Griff asked.

Mrs. Severs nodded. "I do." She lifted the cell phone off the table in front of her and scrolled until she found the number she was looking for. "Here it is." She held it out to Griff.

He saved the number into his cell phone. "Thank you."

"Mr. and Mrs. Severs, I appreciate you taking the time to answer questions about your daughter."

Rachel touched the box. "And thank you for giving me a glimpse into her life. Again, I'm so sorry for your loss."

"We go through our lives one day at a time," Mrs. Severs said. "It's the best we can do when we still hurt for her."

Rachel and Griff stood.

Griff shook hands with Mr. Severs. "Thank you both for inviting us in." The two men walked toward the gate.

Mrs. Severs followed with Rachel by her side. "We hope you have better luck finding the one responsible for what happened to Christy."

"We're working it," Rachel said. "Can't make any guarantees, but we will do our best."

The two Severs nodded.

"Thank you for trying," Mr. Severs said.

Griff led the way through the gate and out to where he'd parked the truck on the street.

When they were back on the road heading toward Fool's Gold, Griff glanced over at Rachel. "Are you going to call Bryan Peterson, or do you want me to make that connection?"

"You're driving," she said, shaking her head. "I'll do it."

He handed her his cell phone and returned his hands to the steering wheel, navigating heavy traffic.

Rachel keyed in the number and pressed *Send*. After the fourth ring, his voicemail engaged.

Rachel left a message. "Hello, Bryan. This is Deputy Rachel West from Fool's Gold, Colorado. When you get a minute, please call me in reference to Christy Severs. Thank you." She ended the call but kept his cell phone in her palm.

"Do you want to drive up to Denver and meet Bryan in person?" Griff asked.

Rachel shook her head. "No, I think we can accomplish what we need to do without disrupting his family."

Her cell phone rang. She glanced at the caller ID. "It's Bryan." Rachel answered, "This is Deputy West."

"Hi. This is Bryan Peterson. You have questions about Christy Severs?"

"Yes, sir," Rachel said. "I'm going to send a photo of a necklace to you. Can you tell me if you gave it to Christy a couple of days before you proposed?"

"Maybe," Bryan said. "It's been a while. I can't remember my name half the time, much less what I've given people over the years."

Rachel texted the images of the heart-shaped necklace with the inscriptions on the front and back to Bryan.

He sent his response pretty quickly. "Not mine. I would never have said *Until death do us part.*"

"Why?" Rachel asked. "It's part of the usual marriage ceremony."

"It's not at all classy. You want to go into marriage

thinking you'll be together all the way into your nineties," Bryan said.

"Did Christy ever complain about anyone stalking, following or bothering her in any way?"

"Man, you're asking me to remember back that far. Seems to me she had some guy at the restaurant where she worked try to ask her out on several occasions. The guy wouldn't take no for an answer. She said she handled things by herself."

"Do you remember his name?" Rachel asked.

"No," Bryan said. "I just remember he was a customer, not a co-worker. I'd say ask one of the other staff members at the restaurant, but I think the restaurant changed names and ownership in the past fifteen years. I doubt the same people work there."

"Thank you, Bryan," Rachel said. "If you think of anything else, you have my number."

"I hope you find who did this," Bryan said. "I think about Christy every time I look at my daughter. Thankfully, my wife understands. Christy was my first love. She'll always have a special place in my heart. Don't get me wrong...I love Lisa very much and feel blessed to have her as my life partner. However, Christy was an amazing woman and deserved to have a long and beautiful life. I hope you get the guy who killed her. I don't think they did enough fifteen years ago."

"We'll do our best," Rachel promised and ended the call.

"I'm heading back to Fool's Gold," Griff said.

"Good. I want to check something at my apartment."

"About your apartment..." Griff looked her way for a second and then returned his attention to the busy road ahead. "I think you need to stay somewhere else until we can get the locks rekeyed."

She grinned. "I can always go old-school and jam a chair under the door handle. And I have a bodyguard protecting me. What more do I need?"

Griff's lips pressed into a thin line. "We need to pay a visit to Lost Valley Ranch, where the Brotherhood Protectors offices are. I'd like to see what we have available that could make our job easier."

"After we go to my apartment, we can stop by the hardware store to buy new locks for my door. After that, we can head out to Lost Valley Ranch," Rachel's eyebrows rose. "Sound like a plan?"

He nodded. "Sounds good."

Griff drove through Ute Pass, following the curvy road past towering rock walls. As they neared Fool's Gold, the terrain smoothed into rolling hills with the incredible backdrop of fourteen-thousand-foot peaks topped with caps of snow.

"I see why Lindsay loved it here so much." Rachel stared at the amazing scenery, imagining her sister's delight at the beauty all around. "It's stunning."

"Yes, it is," Griff said. "I wasn't sure I would stay when I promised to come here for the interview."

"I quit my job in San Diego to come here. Not for the view, but to keep the search for my sister's killer alive."

He slowed to turn off Main Street, heading north toward Rachel's apartment complex. "But now that you're here, will you ever return to California and your career as a highway patrol officer?"

"I hadn't thought past the investigation." Her brow dented. "But yes. I think I will stay. There's so much to do here, and most of it is outdoors. Besides, Sheriff Faulkner needs me."

Griff chuckled. "And half a dozen more deputies."

"What about you?" Rachel faced him and cocked an eyebrow. "Are you out of here when the job is done? Or will you stay working for Brotherhood Protectors?"

"Like you, I haven't given it much thought. I want all my focus to be on keeping you safe." He laid his hand on the console, palm up.

Rachel laid her hand across his, and he closed his fingers around hers. She liked how warm and strong his fingers were and imagined how they'd feel roaming over every inch of her body.

Heat rose from low in her belly, up her torso through her breasts and shot up her neck into her cheeks. Yeah, she'd been in a long, dry spell for a while, not interested in sex just for sex until she'd met Griff.

Now, she wanted all the sex, over and over. Not with some random guy. She wanted Griff.

And with her desire mounting, so too did her guilt. She shouldn't fixate on her own needs. She should be solely focused on finding her sister's killer. The guy had stolen her life yet was living his own, free from consequences.

Tamping down the heat at her core, she squared her shoulders.

When Griff pulled into the parking lot of her apartment complex, Rachel was once again in control of her thoughts, actions focused. She was out of the truck heading for her unit before Griff could shift into park and follow.

He caught up quickly, his long strides eating the distance between them. "I guess I'm going to have to run to keep up with you."

"I want this to be over. It's been six months since Lindsay's death. Fifteen years since Christy's. It's been long enough." She jammed her key into the lock and twisted. "I don't know why I even locked the door. It didn't slow him down one damned bit." Her anger burned so hotly that her hands shook as she pushed open the door. "I just want to get my hands on him and make him pay for what he did."

"Hey." Griff laid his hands gently on her shoulders and turned her to face him. "We're going to get him. Between your exceptional investigative skills and all the people working to see this through, it's going to happen."

"I don't want my sister's case to be like Christy's." She looked up into his eyes, her heart squeezing so hard inside her chest she could barely breathe. "Fifteen years," she whispered. "Her parents have suffered for fifteen years."

"Sadly, they'll continue to suffer for the rest of their lives. They'll never get over the loss of their daughter."

"But capturing the killer will bring closure to that chapter of their lives. Then they can concentrate on the good memories they made with Christy."

"And you think by capturing the killer, you'll be able to focus on the good memories you had with Lindsay?"

Rachel nodded. "At least then, I'll have stopped her attacker from taking another innocent life. I can't rest until that happens. Lindsay would want him brought to justice. I want that, too."

Griff brushed a strand of her hair away from the bump on her forehead. "We'll do this as long as you don't sacrifice your safety in the process."

"I can't make any guarantees," she said. "I'll do whatever it takes to bring that bastard out into the open and take him off the streets of Fool's Gold and Colorado Springs."

"That's a tall order to fill for someone the state and local police weren't able to identify."

"It wasn't their sister or daughter. They aren't feeling the pain."

"What did you need from your apartment?" Griff asked.

Rachel headed for her bedroom. "I needed to check on something.

"When you're done, pack a go-bag," Griff said, "you should put together everything you'll need for a couple of days."

"I don't need to stay elsewhere. I like having my things around me."

Griff touched a finger to her lips. "We'll play it by ear. If I think it's too dangerous for you to be in the middle of everything, I'll drag your ass out." he grinned. "How's that sound?"

She grinned. "I have an image of you throwing me over your shoulder like a sack of potatoes."

He waggled his brows. "I can do that," he said. He pointed to his left shoulder. "With this shoulder. The other one has a way to go in recovery."

Rachel leaned up on her toes and pressed her lips to his. "And there I go breaking my own rules, again. I'd better get done with what I need to do before you go all caveman on me." She stepped through the door and waited for him to run a quick check of her apartment.

When he gave her the all-clear thumbs-up, she hurried into her bedroom and flung open her closet. On the upper shelf was a big cardboard box, much like the one the Severs kept with all of what was left of Christy's life packed inside. Only this was what was left of Lindsay's life, besides the memories Rachel kept dear to her heart.

Rachel laid Lindsay's box on the bed and removed items one at a time. She'd donated much of her sister's clothing to a homeless shelter, only choosing to keep a few items that meant a lot to Lindsay.

She laid out a denim ball cap with the words "Key West" embroidered in bright pink. Lindsey had saved it from the trip Rachel and Lindsay had taken two years ago. That had been before she'd moved to Colorado and met her boyfriend.

An artist's journal was included in the box with little drawings and watercolors on every page. Rachel had considered having some of them framed. But she hadn't been ready to tear pages out of Lindsay's book.

Like Christy, Lindsay had a jewelry box with earrings, rings and necklaces.

Rachel removed the jewelry box and opened it carefully. Inside were drawers for rings, another for earrings and a side panel where Lindsay had draped her necklaces.

Rachel sifted through all of them, strangely relieved she didn't find what she suspected might be there. As she placed the jewel box back in the bottom of the cardboard box, her breath lodged in her throat.

A flash of Tiffany blue caught her attention in the

far corner of the box beneath what had been one of Lindsay's favorite silk scarves.

Her hand shaking, Rachel pulled the scarf out of the box. Beneath it lay a small blue box, exactly like the one she'd found on the floor of her apartment that morning.

"She got one, too?" a deep voice said behind her.

Rachel jumped. "Geez, Griff!" She'd been so caught up in the items from Lindsay's box, she'd almost forgotten Griff was in her apartment.

His hands settled on her shoulders, massaging them gently. "Let's see what's inside it."

"We already know." Still, she had to open the box to verify.

Inside, nestled against a bed of blue satin, lay a shiny silver heart on a thin silver chain.

"Same inscription?" Griff asked.

Rachel nodded.

I LOVE YOU on one side.

UNTIL DEATH DO US PART on the other.

"You came back here to find the one he gave your sister," Griff said.

Rachel nodded, staring down at the necklace in her hand. "I hadn't gone through her jewelry box. I wasn't ready. And it was here all along."

"To me, the necklaces remove all doubt. You're truly a target, and we're dealing with a serial killer or a copycat of the one who killed Christy."

A chill slithered across the back of Rachel's neck.

So, she was a target.

A target who could potentially lure the killer out into the open.

She lifted her chin and met Griff's gaze. "Fuck him. As far as I'm concerned, it's game on."

CHAPTER 8

GRIFF DROVE in silence to the Lost Valley Ranch, his mind going over everything that had happened and the information they'd uncovered that day. Had he only been in Fool's Gold for twenty-four hours?

He shook his head.

"Why are you shaking your head?" Rachel asked.

"There's so much that has happened, and so much we don't know. I like having a better understanding of my enemy than I have right now."

Rachel snorted, "I like knowing who he is. This not knowing is wearing on my last nerve. I've been here for three months. Why has he chosen now to come after me? He must've been my stalker in the shadows. But he hadn't made a move."

"Until I showed up on the scene, and we announced that we were engaged."

Rachel's brow dipped into a V. "Christy had just

gotten engaged. Lindsay had, too, when they were attacked. And the wedding veil could be his way of boasting that he'd kept them from getting married or saying he'd married them." She shook her head. "I don't know. The man's crazy. There's no telling what's going on in his warped and dangerous mind."

"What doesn't make sense was for him to run you off the road," Griff said. "His M.O. is to strangle his victims with a wedding veil."

"Unless he planned on strangling me once he'd forced me to crash," Rachel pointed out.

Griff pulled through the gate to Lost Valley Ranch and drove up to the lodge. The sun teetered on the edge of the mountain peaks, casting long shadows across the ground.

People were gathered in front of the lodge, sitting on the deck in various rocking chairs, porch swings and lounge chairs. A couple of men stood beside a large grill. Smoke rose from inside it as a man with a barrel chest and a shock of gray hair opened the grill. He laughed at something the man beside him said and turned toward Griff's truck as he shifted into park.

"Looks like they're having a party," Rachel said. "I hate to barge in unannounced. I think we'll be all right at my apartment for the night."

Griff shook his head. "Jake said they had rooms set aside for members of the team. Your apartment isn't safe." He got out of the truck and came around to her side.

Rachel was already down from her seat and closing the door.

He held out his hand.

Rachel took it and allowed him to lead her toward the group.

He liked holding her hand. It was strong, yet feminine and warm, not cold like so many women he'd met.

JAKE COGBURN DESCENDED THE STEPS, carrying a tray of raw hamburgers. "Just in time. Gunny didn't feel like cooking in the kitchen, so we're doing it outside."

"It's a beautiful evening for it," Rachel said.

Jake smiled down at her and held out his hand. "I'm glad to see you're feeling better."

"Thank you," she said as she shook his hand.

"Are you giving Griff a run for his money trying to keep up with you?" Jake grinned and shook hands with Griff.

"Not really," she said. "I need to step up my game."

Griff liked that she had a sense of humor, even when she'd become the target of a serial killer.

"We hope you've come to stay here until the killer is caught." A woman with sandy-blond hair pulled back into a ponytail joined them. "Hi, I'm RJ Tate. I know I've run into you in town a few times, but I don't think we've actually been introduced. You're the new deputy in town."

Rachel nodded. "Yes, ma'am."

Jake slipped his arm around RJ and pulled her close. "RJ is my fiancé. She and her father, Gunny, are the owners and operators of the Lost Valley Ranch and the Watering Hole. RJ, this is Griff, the newest member of the Brotherhood Protectors."

RJ held out her hand and gave his a firm shake. "I've heard a lot about you. You'll be a welcome addition to the team."

"Thank you."

"GUNNY, say hello to Rachel and Griff," RJ called out.

The gray-haired man raised his spatula. "Hello!" Then he flipped the burgers on the grill, added more and closed the top again. "Grab a beer. Chow will be ready soon."

Jake led Griff and Rachel to a large tin tub full of ice, beer and sodas. "Choose your poison."

Rachel leaned down, snagged a longneck bottle of beer and twisted off the cap.

Griff did the same and downed a long swallow of the cool brew.

"Come meet some of the gang," Jake said. "All of them are former special operations, whether they were Navy SEALS, Delta or Rangers."

He stood at the base of the steps leading up to the porch and said in a loud, clear voice, "Hey, listen up."

Everyone stopped talking and turned toward Jake.

"This is John Griffin, Navy SEAL, recently separated from active duty. He's our newest recruit to the team. With him is one of Teller County's finest, Deputy Rachel West."

Griff raised a hand. "You can call me Griff."

Jake pointed to a man with blond hair, cut high and tight. He stood with his arm around a woman a foot shorter than him with rich brown hair and brown eyes.

"Max Thornton, former Army 10th Special Forces."

Max shook Griff's hand. "Welcome aboard."

"With Max," Jake continued, "is JoJo Barrera-Ramirez. She's prior Army and one of the finest mechanics I know. She can fix anything."

"Anything mechanical, but I'm hopeless at fixing my hair," she said with a crooked grin. "Nice to meet you, Griff."

Jake nodded toward a tall man with black hair and blue eyes above them, leaning against a porch rail. "Cage Weaver, former Army Ranger."

Weaver nodded and tipped his head toward the auburn-haired woman standing beside him. "This is my fiancé, Emily Strayhorn."

Jake smiled at the redhead. "Emily is a mental health therapist at the VA hospital in Colorado

Springs. She plays a vital role in helping our guys and gals dealing with PTSD."

He pointed to the tallest man, who had brown hair and brown eyes and a thick shadow of stubble across his chin. "Griff, you might be familiar with Navy SEAL Sawyer Johnson. I believe you two served together at some point in your careers."

"We did," Griff nodded. "Good to reconnect."

"I believe you saved my ass in Afghanistan."

Griff chuckled. "Someone had to. You were knee-deep on Taliban."

"And out of ammo." Sawyer shook his head. "Never was happier to see a friendly face." He turned to the woman leaning against him. "This is the love of my life, Kinsley Brothers, a physician assistant at the VA hospital."

"Can you wrap this up?" Gunny said. "Food's ready."

Jake grinned and named the other men, pointing at them one by one. "Enzo Ramos, Bryce Coleman, Tayo Perez. You can get to know each other after we eat. Gunny waits chow for no one."

Everyone moved into the lodge's dining room and gathered around the long table nearest the kitchen. The food was laid out on a buffet for the lodge guests and the Brotherhood team.

After filling their plates, everyone claimed a seat. The food was great and the conversations lively, with men and women contributing to the humor and discussion.

Griff caught up with Jake and Sawyer and spoke with the former Army Special Operations teammates for the first time since the crash.

Kinsley Brothers leaned past Sawyer to smile at Rachel. "I saw your SUV when the tow truck was pulling it out of the ditch." She shook her head. "You're lucky to be alive."

Rachel nodded. "I was lucky Griff found me and helped me get out."

"When we're done with supper," Jake said. "We can adjourn to the Brotherhood offices in the basement and go over what we've learned today."

Griff was glad to wait until their meal was over. Ever since they'd found the third necklace among Lindsay's things, a heavy weight had settled in his chest. He wondered if he could keep Rachel safe from the Wedding Veil Killer. The man had proven to be clever and thorough in his ability to erase his presence.

As the meal drew to a close, the men and women collected plates and glasses.

Jake walked with Griff to the kitchen. "One of the rules of engagement we made with Gunny for allowing us to use his lodge as a base for our regional operations was that when our guys aren't on assignment, they're tasked to help out around the lodge.

That way, things get done here, and the guys are gainfully employed."

Griff nodded. "And you probably want to know if I agree to the terms?"

Jake smiled. "Yes."

He nodded. "I do."

"Any experience with livestock, horseback riding or operating an ATV in challenging terrain?" Jake asked.

Griff gave the man a half-smile as he used his shoulder to push open the swinging door into the kitchen. "I didn't grow up on a ranch, but I spent many summers at my uncle's farm east of San Diego. I have some great memories of those summers, riding horses, swimming in the creek and taking care of fences and livestock. I can help around the lodge and love it."

Jake nodded. "Good deal. Oh, by the way, helping out at the lodge includes helping with Gunny's Watering Hole. The bar and grill."

"I've flipped a burger or two in my teens," Griff said. "I've never been a bartender, but I can learn."

"If you can make sandwiches, clean tables and deliver drinks, you qualify." Jake chuckled. "The job description for a Brotherhood Protector is varied and fluid. We do whatever we have to in order to provide the service and protection our clients need."

"You've really bought into this Brotherhood Protector gig," Griff said.

Jake nodded. "Never thought I would. Hell, I was ready to check out of life when Kujo showed up and pulled me out of the bottle I'd sunk so deeply into. My work through this organization has shown me that I can still be a vital part of a community. Many people need me as much as I need them. The only regret I have is that I didn't come to work for the Brotherhood any earlier than I did."

"I'm glad to hear you're making it work and are happy," Griff said.

"A lot of guys who leave active duty never find that happy place and end up shooting themselves before the end of the first year. I was almost one of them." He tapped his prosthetic device. "Now, I'm okay with who I am and what I can and can't do."

"I'm happy for you," Griff said. "RJ seems perfect for you."

"She's amazingly smart and driven. The scary part is that she doesn't need me." Jake's lips quirked upward. "It's refreshing being with a woman who can hold her own. And she *wants* to be with me. I'm a lucky man."

Everyone pitched in to clean the dishes, dry them and put them away. The kitchen was spotless by the time they cleared out.

"When your guys are done in your offices, I could use some help over at the Watering Hole," Jake said.

"We'll cover for Gunny," RJ said. "The bar will be busy with people attending this weekend's town founders parade and activities. The overflow of visitors looking for a drink in Fool's Gold will find their way out here. The day shift's about ready to leave. I'll head over with Gunny and relieve the folks who need to get home to their families."

Gunny and RJ left through the front door.

Jake held up a hand. "I'd like my team to convene in the basement in five minutes. Ladies, make yourselves at home, or you can join the men in the basement."

"I'm coming with you," JoJo said.

Emily raised a hand. "Me, too."

"I'm not hanging out on the porch by myself," Kinsley said. "I'm coming, too."

Rachel slipped her hand into Griff's. "I think I need to be with you in the basement. If there's a discussion of the investigation, I definitely need to be in the middle of it."

He squeezed her hand gently. "That's fine. I want you with me at all times."

"Surely, the Wedding Veil Killer wouldn't come to a crowded lodge and attempt to kill me with so many witnesses." She shook her head. "He's been too careful not to be seen or leave any marks."

"I think it's like you said." Griff tipped his head. "He's walking, living and laughing among us. We can't see him because he's just a normal Joe. Someone everyone trusts and sees every day without really seeing him." He gave her a twisted grin. "Know anyone like that?"

Rachel rolled her eyes. "Half the people in town fit that description. Everyone gets so busy in their own lives they don't pay attention to the nuances of the people around them." She grimaced. "That includes me."

"You've been watching everyone, studying them," Griff said.

"Yeah, but am I watching the right one? How will I know? How do profilers do it? How do they get into a killer's head?"

Jake approached Griff. "Follow me. I'll show you our base of operations." He led them through the kitchen to a door at the far end that opened onto stairs leading down into a basement.

As Jake descended the stairs, lights came on automatically. The long room lit up bright and white. It had been tastefully transformed from a regular basement to a sleek, modern office with a long conference table, a large LED screen at one end and a bank of computers with an array of monitors.

"Nice," Griff said.

Jake grinned. "Wait until you see the armory." He walked across the floor to a door with a biometric scanner. Jake touched his finger on the scanner. Moments later, the lock made a clicking sound.

With a flourish, Jake swung the door open to a room filled with an impressive array of weapons, from AR-15s to nun-chucks. Handguns lined the walls in every size and configuration. A large cabinet stood in the center of the room with drawers on both sides.

Jake pulled open one of the spacious drawers, exposing helmets with night vision goggles. In another drawer were armored vests and gloves.

The last drawer contained a variety of communications devices and trackers.

"You might want to tag Ms. West with a tracker in case something happens and we lose her." He held up a necklace that had an ornate, oval-shaped pendant.

"I'll take it." Rachel reached for the necklace. "There's nothing like being the target of a serial killer to make you want people to creep on you."

Jake pulled out a handheld tracking device and turned it on, showing them how to use it.

"The best scenario is to not lose Rachel," Griff said.

"True," Jake said. "No matter how hard you try to control your environment, things happen. It's better to be prepared for the worst and have nothing happen than to be unprepared when it does."

Everyone gathered around the conference table.

"Not all of my guys are here tonight, but all are available if we need them," Jake said. "And for that matter, all of Hank's guys in Montana can be mobilized should we need them."

Griff and Rachel spent the next five minutes

bringing the team up to date on the status of their investigation, showing them the heart-shaped necklace and discussing the fifteen-year-old cold case of Christy Severs.

"Neither Christy nor Lindsay were raped. Without witnesses, fingerprints or any other DNA evidence, we can't identify our perp," Rachel said. "Christy was murdered in a back alley at night. No one saw it happen. My sister was killed on an isolated mountain trail with nobody around."

"The feds should consider this a serial killing if he's killed at least three victims," Rachel said. "I don't want to let him kill again."

JoJo shook her head. "Especially considering his gift to you this morning. My friend, you're his next target."

Griff's hands tightened into fists. "We can't let it happen."

"And we won't," Jake assured them.

"What about security cameras at your apartment," Tayo asked. "Could we review the footage from around the time he delivered your necklace?"

Rachel shook her head. "The security cameras were down at the apartment complex when he delivered the gift."

"Convenient," Max murmured.

Jake nodded. "Makes you wonder if he tampered with them."

"The FBI won't take on a serial killing case with

only two victims at this point," Rachel said. "But he's established an M.O. with the first two killings, and he's sent the gift to me."

"Why the gap between the first and second?" Sawyer asked. "And now it's been six months since your sister's death. Why now?"

Griff frowned. "Christy's mother mentioned a couple of times that her daughter looked a lot like Rachel."

Rachel nodded. "Although Lindsay and I were half-sisters, we looked like we could be twins. We had different fathers, but we took after our mother. It could be the killer has issues with women who look like us."

"Other than looks, what else do all three of you have in common?" Jake asked.

"Christy and Lindsay were engaged, which is in keeping with the wedding veil angle," Emily said. "But that doesn't hold true for Rachel."

Griff and Rachel exchanged a look.

"Actually," Rachel said, "to explain Griff's sudden presence in my life, and so he could stay in my room at the hospital, we made it public that we'd just gotten engaged."

"How soon after Lindsay and Christy were engaged were they murdered?" JoJo asked.

Griff's gut knotted. "The next day for both."

"He likes women who look like Rachel," Emily said. "And he doesn't like it when they choose to marry someone other than him. He might have thought he had a chance with them, then feels betrayed when they say yes to someone else. It makes him angry. I'd bet my certification that he will make a move soon."

Rachel's gaze met Griff's.

He'd promised to keep her safe and help her find the man who'd killed her sister.

He hoped like hell they found the guy before he added another tick mark toward becoming an FBI serial killer.

Before he murdered Rachel.

CHAPTER 9

RACHEL SHOWERED and changed into a loose T-shirt and shorts, her usual attire to sleep in. As she glanced at herself in the mirror, she regretted that she didn't have a sexy lingerie set.

Then she chuckled softly. She'd never wanted a sexy nightie before she'd met Griff. He knew she was a law enforcement officer, an expert marksman and working in a male-dominated career. Most guys would be intimidated or consider her too masculine. Not Griff. He seemed to like her the way she was. And she liked him. He made her feel…feminine. Not all soft and girly. More like strong and sexy… completely aware of her body and how it would fit with his.

She touched a hand to her breast, surprised at how quickly her heart beat at just the thought of their bodies fitting together.

RJ had settled her in a room on the second floor. The room had a French door leading out onto the upper deck.

Griff had been assigned the room beside hers. If she had any trouble, all she had to do was yell, and he'd come running.

Rachel liked it better when he'd been in the same room with her. Not that she was afraid to be alone. Yeah, he turned her on, and she'd like to do more with Griff than kiss and hold hands. More than that, she liked being with him. His presence made her feel less alone. More complete. She realized that had been what was missing in her life all along.

She'd dated other men and had never felt like that with them. The first time she'd met Griff at McP's, she'd felt something special. If she had it her way, she wouldn't let him get away again.

Still keyed up from all that had happened in the past twenty-four hours, Rachel left the bathroom, crossed to the French door and pulled it open. She stepped onto the upper deck and lifted her face to the cool breeze.

Starlight shone down from the heavens. The majestic mountain peaks towered around the lodge, indigo blue against the night sky.

She listened for sounds of movement in the room beside hers but heard none. Had Griff gone back downstairs to talk more with the men of his new team?

Walking out on the upper deck, Rachel had secretly hoped Griff would come out at the same time.

After ten minutes of breathing cool mountain air and staring out at the star-studded heavens, Rachel retreated to her bedroom and slid beneath the sheets.

The calm of the mountain setting and crispness of the air must have done the trick. Within a few short minutes, she drifted to sleep.

Her dreams started out nice.

She stood on a trail on the side of a mountain, looking out over the vast beauty of the Colorado Rockies. Skies so blue were dotted with puffy white clouds. She walked on, the trail growing steeper, the ground more uneven as she went. Rounding a bend in the trail placed her in the shadow of the mountain. The clouds turned gray, and the blue skies darkened.

Footsteps sounded behind Rachel, but every time she turned around, the trail behind her was empty. She climbed faster, her breathing becoming more labored, the altitude and fear pressing against her chest.

The footsteps behind her came faster.

To stay ahead, Rachel ran, her feet slipping on loose gravel, her lungs burning with each breath. She raced to the top of an incline and slid to a stop when she realized the trail ended in a three-thousand-foot drop-off. With a rock wall on one side and a slope so steep and long on the other that she would tumble to her death, she had only one way to go.

Rachel turned to face her pursuer.

He stood in the deepest shadows, dressed in black and his face hidden. In his hands, he carried a snowy-white wedding veil.

He stepped forward, one foot at a time, his face no more visible even as he moved closer.

Rachel knew she'd have to fight her way past him to escape. She braced herself as best she could on the uneven ground and charged like a bull toward the man and the veil.

She hit him hard, shoving him back along the trail. He staggered, regained his footing and grabbed her arms.

He was bigger and stronger than her. She couldn't give up hope. She had to take him down, had to stop him from killing her so that he couldn't kill others.

He trapped her arms to her sides and wrapped the veil around her throat.

That's when she decided, if she couldn't fight her way free, she'd take him with her.

As the veil tightened around her throat, Rachel changed the direction of her struggle, twisted and backed into the killer, shoving him toward the edge of the trail.

He fought to keep from falling.

Rachel strained against his weight. Just a little more.

He tipped over the edge and fell down the steep slope, still holding the veil wrapped around her throat, pulling Rachel with him.

As she fell toward her death, she closed her eyes and thought, "This is a dream...it's not real."

Rachel woke in a cold sweat, the sheets tangled around her so tightly she couldn't move and her heart pounding so hard she could barely breathe. The panic of falling to her death in her dream transferred to being trapped in the sheets. She tore at the sheets, finally kicking her feet free. Then she leaped out of bed to stand barefoot on the cool wood floor.

Adrenaline pumping, she had to keep moving. She crossed to the French doors, pulled them open and stepped out onto the porch. She'd paced to the end of the long deck before her heartbeat slowed and she had her breathing under control. When she turned around to go back to her room, she froze, and her heart lodged in her throat.

A shadowy figure stood between her and the door to her room. Fear wrapped its icy fingers around her heart, and she was back in the dream. "No," she whispered. She turned to run only to realize she was at the end of the porch, boxed in by the railing.

She spun toward the first set of doors nearest her, grabbed the handle and tried to open it. It was locked.

The figure moved toward her, closing the distance one step at a time.

"No," she whispered. "You won't get me this time." Rachel bunched her fists and waited for him to come to her. She'd fight him with all her might. He wouldn't best her this time.

"Rachel," a deep, familiar voice sounded in the darkness.

Thinking her mind was playing tricks on her, Rachel maintained her defensive stance, preparing to throw the first punch.

"Rachel, sweetheart, it's me, Griff." As the shadowy figure moved closer, the starlight glinted on his face.

Her body poised to fly at the enemy, she launched herself forward and hit him with the full weight of her body. At the same time, realization hit her.

Griff staggered backward, grabbed for a brace post and stopped his and Rachel's fall before they hit the floor. Then he wrapped his arms around her and held her, stroking her hair and back. "Hey, hey. It's okay. It's just me."

She pressed her face against his naked chest, her body trembling with relief. "I thought you were the killer."

"Well, now you know I'm not. You're okay. He's not here."

"I was dreaming," she said, her voice muffled against his chest. "I was my sister, hiking along a mountain trail. He was following me. I ran, but the trail ended."

"Shh," Griff's soothing voice helped calm her.

"He tried to strangle me with the veil. I pushed us both off the trail. We were falling when I woke up."

"Now, you're safe with me." He tipped her chin up

and brushed his lips across her forehead. "I'm not going to let him hurt you." He pressed a kiss to the tip of her nose. "And good for you for pushing him off the cliff. Though I'd rather you hadn't fallen with him."

"I couldn't let him win," she whispered, mesmerized by the starlight glinting off his light blue eyes.

"That's my girl." This time, he brushed his lips across hers. "You're the baddest badass I know."

She wanted more than just a brush of a kiss. "Now, you're teasing me," she said, her pulse picking up again—this time for an entirely different reason.

His lips quirked. "Is it working?"

She nodded, her body becoming increasingly aware of how tightly she was pressed to him. The chill mountain air did nothing to cool the heat building at her core and spreading through her veins.

A shiver of anticipation rippled through her.

"Cold?" Griff backed away. "We should get you back to your room. You're not dressed for this temperature."

"You're right." She was overdressed for her body temperature. "We should go inside."

Griff slipped his arm around her waist and guided her toward her room. Rachel stopped when they reached the open door, her heart racing again.

"Afraid you'll step back into your nightmare?" he asked, his breath stirring the tendrils of hair near her ear.

She nodded. "It was so real."

He reached inside, grabbed the door handle and pulled it closed. "You can stay in my room."

She let him lead her toward his open door and into his room.

"I can sleep on the chair," he said.

"No. This is your room, you're big, and I'm not. I'll sleep in the chair."

Griff closed the door behind him and twisted the lock. Then he turned, scooped her up in his arms and deposited her on the bed. "I'll take the chair," he said.

Rachel wrapped her arm around his neck before he could back away. "I'll sleep here on one condition..." She stared up into his eyes. "You sleep with me." While she tried to look confident and secure in her desirability, her breath caught and held, afraid of his response. What if he wasn't attracted to her? Her confidence slipped, and heat rose up her neck into her cheeks. "Unless you're not interested in sleeping with me. In that case, forget it. I'll sleep in my own room." She started to get up but couldn't with Griff still leaning over her. "Seriously, I shouldn't have come on to you. You're my bodyguard. I shouldn't have suggested we sleep together. It can only cause a whole lot of trouble."

Griff grinned and crushed her mouth with his, stopping her from making an even bigger fool of herself.

Oh, and his lips were so fine and hot and...

Rachel opened to him and met his tongue in a battle of desire, both thrusting and parrying until they were forced to call a truce and come up for air.

"You're right; I'm your protector. And you're wrong about my not being interested." He pressed another kiss to her lips. "I'm so interested, I'm afraid."

"You? Afraid?" She blinked up at him. "Of what?"

"Of blowing it."

"I don't understand. Are you afraid you will lose your position with the Brotherhood Protectors if you sleep with me?"

He laughed. "No. That's not what scares me. I'm afraid of losing my focus on the danger surrounding you. I'm afraid I'll let my concentration slip just long enough for that killer to get to you." He rested his forehead against hers. "I'm afraid of failing you and losing you forever. I can't let that happen. I won't."

She looked into his eyes, her heart swelling with all the feelings she had for this man. "You care about me?"

"More than you know." He laughed. "More than I ever thought possible."

"I care about you," she said. "Sleep with me."

"I can't."

Her brow wrinkled. "Why?"

"Because I wouldn't sleep," he said, his voice lower, more intense.

Her mouth curved upward. "Who needs sleep anyway?"

He stared down at her for a long moment.

"Good grief, Griff," she said, her patience slipping. "What do I have to do? Spell it out?"

He nodded. "I don't want any misunderstandings about what you want."

She gripped his cheeks between her palms and met his gaze. "Stay with me. Make love to me. Damn it! I want you, John Griffith."

His lips spread into a smile. "It's not nice to curse."

She frowned, finding the man too sexy for his own good and downright maddening. "Then quit teasing me, and let's do this." She planted her hands on his chest and shoved him over to lie on his back. Starting at his lips, she kissed, nipped and tongued her way across his chin, down the length of his throat and lower.

She captured one of his hard brown nipples in her mouth and nipped the button tip.

"Hey." He gripped her arms. "Let me show you how it's done." He winked and rolled her over onto her back.

She gave him a wicked smile. "It's about time."

He repeated the pattern of her path on her lips, chin and down her neck.

When he reached for the hem of her shirt, Rachel brushed his hands aside and rolled him off her. Ready to be skin-to-skin with the man and not waste another moment, she yanked her T-shirt over her head and flung it across the room. Her shorts went next, followed by her panties.

He lay on his side, his head propped in his hand, chuckling. "You're stealing some of my fun. Undressing you is like opening a present. Half the fun is in the anticipation. It's called foreplay."

She pressed her lips together. "My body is already on fire. Shut up and get naked." She reached for his shorts, but he moved away and rolled off the bed.

"Wait," Rachel sat up. "Where are you going? Am I coming on too strong? Damn. I'm rusty at this."

He laughed out loud. "Sweetheart, you're perfect. I just need to get some protection before we lose our minds to lust."

Rachel flopped back against the pillow. "I'm glad someone is thinking."

He claimed a packet from his wallet, shucked his shorts and laid beside her. "You're wound up tighter than a top. Relax. Quit worrying if you're doing it wrong or saying the wrong thing. Just feel."

He traced a finger from her lips, across her chin to her ear, where he tugged gently on her earlobe before brushing across her shoulder with the lightest of touches, moving halfway down her arm. From there, he swept his fingers across her breasts, slowing to tweak the nipples between his thumb and forefinger, rolling the tip into a tight ball.

"Relax, he said," Rachel muttered, the tension

building inside as he played her body like an instrument.

When he replaced his fingers with his lips, the tension shot to a whole new level, sending her on the path to completely losing her mind.

Griff sucked her nipple into his mouth, rolled it with his teeth and flicked it with the tip of his tongue.

Rachel's fingers curled into the comforter as Griff abandoned her breasts and traveled down the length of her torso to the juncture of her thighs.

Griff parted her legs and settled his broad shoulders between them.

Oh, sweet heaven, she was on fire. Her breath caught as he hovered over her, his fingers moving across her sex, one dipping into her slick channel.

Her hips rose to meet that finger.

Griff brushed his thumb across her clit, setting off a chain reaction of sensations that rippled through her.

When he touched his tongue there, Rachel drew up her knees, dug her heels into the mattress and raised her hips to meet him.

He flicked his tongue across that tightly packed bundle of nerves again and again.

Sensations spun out of control, exploding through her body like fireworks.

She dug her fingers into his hair and held on as she shot to the edge and rocketed to the sky.

Her hips pulsed with the force of her release. Rachel rode the wave of her orgasm to the very end, dropping back to the mattress, spent, satisfied and wanting more.

She lay against the comforter and laughed, experiencing the first joy she'd felt since her sister's death.

GRIFF CLIMBED up her body and leaned over her frowning. "That's not quite the response I envisioned."

"It's a happy response." She smiled up at him. "I thought I'd never know happiness again." Rachel drew in a deep breath and let it out again. "That was amazing." Her hand curved around his cheek. "*You* are amazing." She cocked an eyebrow, grabbed the little foil packet he'd rescued from his wallet and held it up. "But is that all you've got?"

He laughed. "Sweetheart, that was only the beginning."

She tore open the packet, rolled it down the length of him and paused to fondle his balls.

"Keep that up, and this will be fast. Too fast."

Her fingers rolled over him a few seconds more before he tore her hand away and pinned it above her head. "I want to take it slow and savor every second I'm inside you."

She shook her head. "I want it hard and fast while

I'm still basking in the glow of an incredible orgasm. So, bring it."

"Demanding, are we?"

"Life's too damned short not to go for what you want. And I'm not versed in sex talk." Rachel gripped his hips and positioned his cock at her entrance.

It was all Griff could do to maintain control. Her bold forthrightness and "lack" of sex talk had him more than halfway to the goal without even being inside her.

He dipped into her wet channel and pulled out. Going in again, he sank deeper, moving slowly to allow her juices to lubricate him and her channel to adjust to his girth.

On his third venture in, her fingers tightened on his ass, and she pulled him toward her hard and fast. He sank all the way in until he was buried to the hilt.

She fit him perfectly; her tight warmth and moistness felt so good he wanted to bask in it, to relish the sensations for just a second

Her fingers dug into him, spurring him to establish a smooth, steady rhythm, in and out. The closer he came to release, the faster he moved until he rocked like a piston, holding onto his last bit of control for as long as he could. When he burst over the edge, he thrust deep and held, his cock pulsing, heart racing.

Rachel wrapped her legs around him and drew him closer.

Griff lay down on her, milking his release as long as it would last.

Knowing he was crushing the air from her lungs, he rolled her with him to their sides and held her close, relishing the intimate connection, feeling like he'd finally come home. Throughout making love to her, he hadn't noticed the usual pain in his leg, so caught up in the moment, it hadn't mattered.

Rachel rested a hand on his chest and pressed her lips to his skin. "That was…"

"Incredible, amazing, mind-blowing?" he offered.

She tilted her head to one side. "Good."

"Good?" He frowned. "Just good?"

Rachel traced a finger around his nipple. "For round one. Let me know when you're up for round two."

He laughed, smacked her naked ass and hugged her tight. "Your sex talk is perfect."

"You think so?" She tipped her head back and smiled up at him. "Wait until I unleash my sweet nothings on you."

"I can't wait," he said.

Her lips twisted. "Me, too. I'll have to come up with them for next time. What is a sweet nothing, anyway?"

"It's whatever you want it to be, babe." He rested his cheek against her silky hair. "You think you can sleep now?"

Rachel yawned and snuggled into his body.

"Maybe. I'll let you know how it goes when we wake in the morning." Another yawn and she was asleep in Griff's arms.

He shook his head, a smile lingering on his lips. Rachel was confident in her experience as a cop, capable of things most women didn't do and so much more. She had a sense of humor, even if it was while they were making love. And she cared deeply about family and the people she considered family.

If he hadn't been sure before, being with her now brought it home to him.

He was in love with Rachel West.

CHAPTER 10

GRIFF WOKE BEFORE RACHEL, his mind racing, searching for ways to reveal the killer's identity. All night long, he'd been basically terrified. He could not fail in this mission. He couldn't lose another person he loved because he hadn't shot the killer first.

Before daylight, he dropped a kiss on Rachel's lips and slid out of bed without waking her. He carried his clothes into the bathroom, where he dressed, shaved and brushed his teeth.

Rachel was still asleep when he left the bathroom. After checking the lock on the French doors, he stood over the bed once more, staring down at the woman he was falling for, hard and fast. He smiled at the thought.

She was special.

Griff had to do everything in his power to keep her safe.

He opened the door into the hallway, twisted the lock and closed it securely behind him. The lodge was wired with security cameras, and there were enough trained men and women around to protect Rachel if the killer tried to get past them to her. Still, Griff hesitated to leave her for even a second. But he needed to see Jake and get in touch with Hank and his computer guy.

He descended the stairs and passed through the great room and dining room into the kitchen.

At first, Griff thought the kitchen was empty. Then Gunny straightened from bending to pull a couple of skillets from a lower cabinet.

"Good morning, Griff." He tipped his head to the left. "Grab a cup of Joe. RJ and JoJo are taking care of the animals, and I've got breakfast under control. Jake and Thorn are already in the war room, working. You're needed down there more than here."

Griff followed his nose to the fragrant coffee urn in the corner of the kitchen and poured a mug full of the fresh black brew. He took a sip, letting hot liquid burn down his throat into his belly, fortifying him for the day to come.

If the killer stayed true to form, he'd be angling for Rachel today.

His coffee mug in hand, he passed Gunny and opened the door to the basement.

Male voices sounded from below. Griff hurried

down the stairs, careful not to spill his coffee. He'd need it to clear his head.

Max Thornton sat at a desk with his hands on a keyboard and an array of monitors in front of him.

Jake stood behind him, speaking to an image on one of the screens in front of him. "She was wearing a wedding dress, but she was strangled by hand, not a wedding veil?" Jake shook his head. "Maybe it's related. The timeframe is right. And just because he strangled two women with a wedding veil doesn't mean he always will. We'll check with the parents of the bride. Are they still in the area?"

"They're still in Colorado Springs. Swede will text the phone number and address." Hank's voice came over the speaker as clearly as if he stood in the room with them, not on a ranch in Montana.

"At this point, we have to follow any potential clue," Jake said. "Something has to give soon. I'm worried about Ms. West."

"So am I," Griff said, joining them in front of the screen with Hank on video conference. "Hank."

"Griff. How's our client?" Hank asked.

"Sleeping," Griff said. "She had a rough night with nightmares about her sister's death."

"I'm glad she's getting some rest. The accident, her sister's death weighing on her, and now, her own death threat. She has to be stressing."

Griff nodded. "I overheard you talking about another victim?"

"A couple of months before Christy Severs' murder, a young bride, Misty Lantz, was murdered at her wedding reception. Strangled, not with a wedding veil, but by hand."

"And you think it's related to the Wedding Veil Killer?" Griff asked.

"It could be. It was in Colorado Springs; the woman had black hair and green eyes and was in her twenties like the others."

"We can check it out today," Jake said. "We're still trying to figure out why the gap in years between killings. Swede ran a scan on the national crime database searching for wedding veil strangulations."

"Anything?" Griff asked.

Hank shook his head. "Lots of black-haired females in their twenties, but none strangled with a wedding veil."

"I had a thought about the gap," Griff said. "What if he couldn't get to women for the past fifteen years?"

"He'd have to have been in a monastery," Jake said.

Griff met Hank's gaze. "Or jail."

"On it." A blond-haired man's face replaced Hank on the monitor.

"Swede," Griff said.

"That you, Griff?" Axel "Swede" Svenson gave Griff a brief smile.

Griff nodded. "It's been a long time."

"Special mission in Somalia?" Swede gave a

crooked grin. "We were lucky we didn't have our asses handed to us on a platter that day."

"Damn right." Griff lifted his chin. "Good to see you well and happy."

Swede's grin slipped. "Yeah. Sorry to hear about your team. They were good men."

Griff only nodded.

"Give me an hour. I might have something on the criminals released in the past six months to a year who served sentences of twelve to fifteen years."

Griff's brows rose. "An hour?"

Swede's lips pressed together. "I know. I'm slipping. Out here. I have work." His face disappeared, and Hank's came on.

"I'll be working with Swede. Anything we find, we'll send your way ASAP."

"I'll send one of my guys to talk to the bride's folks about her murder," Jake said.

"Keep a tight rein on Ms. West," Hank said. "If he's set on a day after the engagement, that means he'll make his move today. Out here."

Hank's image disappeared.

Thorn rose from his seat and stretched. "I'm going to get a cup of coffee and see if I can help with breakfast."

"I'm going to check on Rachel."

"You won't have to go far," a feminine voice said from across the long room.

Griff turned to find Rachel dressed in jeans, a

white T-shirt and a denim jacket. She'd pulled her hair up into a messy bun on top of her head. Her cheeks were flushed a light pink, and her lips were slightly swollen from being kissed so much the night before. The woman didn't need makeup. She had a natural beauty that filled his heart.

Griff's heart swelled as he joined her on the stairs. He wanted to kiss her good morning, but not in front of the others. "Did you sleep well?"

She nodded. "No nightmares. I promised Gunny I'd set the table in the dining room. Wanna help?"

"Of course." Griff followed her up the stairs to the kitchen.

Gunny had two skillets going of scrambled eggs and another with sausage.

JoJo buttered toast while RJ stirred a pot of sausage gravy.

"Someone grab the biscuits from the lower oven and toss them in that basket," Gunny said.

Griff snagged a couple of oven mitts and rescued a tray of fluffy biscuits from the lower oven.

"While you put those in the basket, I'll go set the table." Rachel leaned over his shoulder, her breast brushing against him. "Mmm. Those smell good."

His groin tightened. "Do you know what you're doing to me, woman?" he whispered.

"I can guess." Rachel left the kitchen, chuckling.

Jake and Thorn came up from the basement. "What can we help with?" Thorn asked.

"You can carry the pitchers of juices and milk to the buffet," RJ said as she poured the sausage gravy into a tureen.

Griff only burned his fingers twice, transferring the biscuits from the baking tray to the basket. He carried them into the dining room and set them on the buffet.

He helped Rachel lay out place settings on the big table and the smaller guest tables.

Guests wandered in and helped themselves to coffee and orange juice.

RJ, JoJo and Gunny marched out of the kitchen with the main courses and arranged them on the buffet.

"Eat up," Gunny said.

The lodge staff, including the Brotherhood Protectors, stood back until the guests had served themselves.

Once everyone had a plate, they returned to their tables.

Breakfast was good. Griff went back for seconds of the biscuits and gravy.

"We have a long, busy day at the ranch today," Gunny said. "If you aren't otherwise employed, we could use all the help we can get. Especially tonight at the Watering Hole."

"What's going on?" Griff asked.

"Fool's Gold's annual Founder's Day," RJ said.

"I'd forgotten about that," Rachel said. "I was

ELLE JAMES

supposed to be on duty." She frowned. "I'll touch base with Sheriff Faulkner to see if they need me to step in."

"No," Griff said.

Rachel frowned. "They are shorthanded. It's my job."

"The sheriff specifically said for you to rest up for a couple of days," Griff reminded her. "And I'm betting he wouldn't want you patrolling alone once he finds out you're the next target of a serial killer."

"I can't put my life on hold." Rachel's frown deepened. "We have no idea when he'll make his move."

"My bet is today," Jake said.

"Agreed," Thorn seconded.

"If he doesn't get the opportunity, he'll just wait for another day and another day until he does," Rachel said. "I have to work to pay my bills."

Griff laid his fork on his plate. "You won't need to pay bills if you're dead."

She sighed. "This sucks."

"Yes, it does." RJ tossed her napkin onto her empty plate. "This guy is a twisted bastard who needs to be taken out."

"Honey, you tell us who he is, and we will." Jake leaned back, coffee cup in hand.

"That's the problem," Thorn said. "We don't know who he is."

"Yet." Jake pushed back from the table. "I think we're getting closer. Swede's working the recently paroled and registered violent offenders angles in the area. "Hopefully, we'll get hit."

"I could do the same search at the sheriff's office," Rachel said.

"Swede's already on it." Griff stood and gathered his plate and Rachel's. "Once he's narrowed it down, we can go through the list, touch bases with parole officers and track them down."

"We can send out a couple of our guys to weed through them," Jake said.

"I want to be in any interrogations," Rachel said.

"With parole officers, maybe," Griff said. "I wouldn't want you to get too close to the killer himself."

Rachel's eyes narrowed. "I want to be the one who takes him down."

"If he'd killed someone I loved, I'd want to take him down, too," RJ said.

"We all would feel the same." Jake took RJ's empty plate. "I'll wash dishes if you clear the tables."

"I'll help with the dishes," RJ said.

Everyone helped carry dishes from the big table and the guest tables into the kitchen.

Rachel and Griff cleared the buffet and wiped it clean.

Once the dining room was finished, Rachel said, "I'm going up to brush my teeth."

Griff smiled. "I'm going with you."

They ran up the stairs and into Rachel's room.

Griff kicked the door shut and pulled Rachel into his arms. "I've wanted to do this since I woke up."

"You should have. It would've been a much better way to wake up than to an empty bed."

"You were sleeping so soundly I didn't want to wake you. And I wanted to get Swede working on finding all the possible parolees in the area that might fit our killer."

"I'll let it slide this time," she said and melted against him. "Do you have any regrets about last night?"

"Yes, one."

She leaned back, a frown marring her brow. "Really?"

He brushed a strand of her hair back from her cheek. "I regret that I waited for a fourth date before making love to you out of some stupid sense of chivalry."

She smiled. "A fourth date that didn't happen."

He nodded. "And I regret not calling you after I returned to the States. You could've used a shoulder to lean on when you lost your sister."

She shook her head. "You lost your entire team. You couldn't have helped me."

"You're right. I wasn't in the right frame of mind to help anyone. Still, I would like to have been there for you."

She pressed her forehead to his chest. "You are now. Though I think I'm tough enough to handle a lot, I'm not sure I can handle this on my own. I have no idea which direction he'll come from."

"I'll do my best to be with you always." He tipped her chin up. "You have to do the same."

"It's hard when I've been on my own for so long. I just naturally do things on my own."

"Until we catch the killer, I need you to be with me."

Rachel nodded. "I'll be glad when this is over and we have him in custody. I feel like I can't do anything without looking over my shoulder." She sighed. "But I can't let that get me down. We have work to do to find him." She tipped her head toward her bed. "Do we have time for an encore?"

He gathered her in his arms and kissed her until he was forced to come up for air.

She laughed and shook her head. "I'll take that as a consolation prize, and we don't have time for more mattress gymnastics."

"I want to, but Swede said he'd get back to us in an hour. That hour is up. Can I get a rain check for tonight?"

She nodded. "Though it sounds like we'll be working the Watering Hole until late."

"You're not working anything."

"I'll have you with me at all times," she said. "I would love to help out Gunny and RJ to pay them back for everything they're doing for me."

Griff frowned. "We'll see."

Rachel smiled. "You know we're going to do it. For now, I'm going to brush my teeth, and then we'll go down to the war room and see what Swede has found."

Griff walked to the door. "I'll meet you in the hall in two minutes."

"You're on."

Griff stepped out and waited until Rachel closed and locked the door behind him.

Like Rachel had said... This sucked.

Griff wanted to take his relationship with Rachel to the next level, to woo her properly, take her out on dates and get to know everything there was to know about her.

Her life had gone on hold when the killer she'd been hunting had made her his next target.

He squared his shoulders.

They had to catch the bastard. The sooner they did, the sooner they could get on with living.

As he hurried to brush his teeth, he realized that with all the focus on Rachel and the serial killer, Griff hadn't had time to think about all he'd lost or even the pain in his damaged leg.

There was a lesson in that realization. He should never forget the past, and he wouldn't. But it was behind him. He needed to live in the present in order to have a future. One that might include a beautiful deputy. His number one goal was to keep her alive today so that they might have a future together.

CHAPTER 11

RACHEL BEAT Griff to the hall, having thoroughly brushed her teeth and checked that her hair was still firmly trapped in a messy bun on top of her head.

She didn't have long to wait for Griff to emerge from his room.

They walked silently down the stairs and through the lodge to the kitchen, where they descended yet another set of stairs into the Brotherhood Protectors' war room.

Jake and Thorn were back at the computer talking to Swede on video conference. Jake held several sheets of paper in his hand.

Rachel's heart beat a little faster. Swede had found persons of interest who could potentially be the killer.

Griff and Rachel joined Jake and Thorn in front of the video monitor.

"I take it you found some possibilities?" Griff asked.

Swede nodded. "Jake has the printouts. I narrowed it down to five."

"Just five?" Rachel wanted to be excited. The list was so small and manageable. But what if one of these five men wasn't the killer? Then what? Back to the databases again. She'd spent months going through crime databases. It was a painful part of investigating crimes. Already, it had been fifteen years for Christy's case. She couldn't live on edge for fifteen years, and she didn't want to die.

The only solution was to find the killer and take him out of circulation. A life sentence with no possibility of parole would get him out of commission. The death penalty would be more permanent. Too bad they'd abolished the death penalty in Colorado.

"Look through them," Swede said. "I included their current addresses, their places of employment and the names of their parole officers, with phone numbers to those parole officers."

"Thanks, Swede," Jake said.

"I'm still sifting through a couple of other searches," the big, blond man said. "I'll let you know if anything else comes up."

Rachel nodded. "Thank you."

Swede ended the conference video, and the screen went black.

Jake spread the sheets of paper over the desk

beside Thorn, who waited with his fingers hovering over the keyboard.

"First up is Steven Rutherford." The image on the sheet was of a heavyset man with thick eyebrows, a large nose and thinning hair. "Steve was sentenced to thirty years for rape and assault and battery. He's out on parole for good behavior and living in a halfway house for parolees. "I'll take Steve." Jake set the sheet to the side.

Thorn pointed to the next information sheet. A man with a big head, permanent sneer and thick greasy hair glared back at them from his photograph. "Forty-two-year-old Dathan Ford, assault and battery. Beat his girlfriend with a tire iron. She ended up in the hospital with a fractured cranium, broken arm and the loss of several teeth. It was his third strike. He was sentenced to fifteen years and served all fifteen."

"As evil as he appears," Rachel said, "it can't be him. I'd notice a guy like him in Fool's Gold." She turned to the Rutherford. "Same with the first guy. I'd remember his face. Neither one of these would fade into the background. They scream violence."

Jake laid the next one in front of her.

Rachel's stomach flipped when she saw the image of a man with dirty-blond hair and a boy-next-door face. "I know him."

Griff leaned closer. "Is that the guy you pointed out at the diner as he was entering?"

She nodded. "Trent Morris. He works at the feed store."

"He's thirty-four, accused of statutory rape and abduction," Jake said. "Lives in Manitou Springs with his parents."

"I would never have suspected him of anything." Rachel shook her head. "His features really fade into the woodwork. We'll take him."

"Are you sure?" Jake asked.

"Griff will be with me at all times," Rachel said. "We can check his whereabouts the day my sister died and where he was when Christy was murdered."

The next image was of a man with dark brown hair and brown eyes. There was something familiar about him, but Rachel couldn't put a finger on it.

Thorn read his information aloud. "Thirty-eight-year-old Rodney Alan Smoot, sentenced to forty years for abduction, battery and stalking. Out on parole after fifteen years. His current address is at a small rental house in Colorado Springs."

"We can stop by and talk with his parole officer after we leave Manitou Springs," Griff said.

Jake laid the last sheet of paper in front of them. A man with forgettable features and mouse-brown hair stared out at them. "Forty-eight-year-old Vernon Owen, sentenced to twenty-five years for battery and stalking his ex-girlfriend. Out on parole for good behavior. I can take him."

"That always seems a stretch," Rachel commented.

"Men whose bad behavior lands them in jail, then turn around and get out on good behavior. To me, it's an oxymoron."

"People think they can be reformed," Jake reasoned.

Rachel snorted. "Most violent offenders are also repeat offenders. Letting them out usually means someone else is going to get hurt."

Griff touched a hand to the small of Rachel's back. "We need to get moving to talk with these people and come back early enough to help prepare for tonight's activities."

He held out his hand to Rachel. She rested her smaller hand across his.

Rachel held up a hand. "We'll be in Manitou Springs and then Colorado Springs to talk with parole officers and the suspects themselves if they're home. And we'll get back here in time to help out in the lodge and the Watering Hole." She smiled at Griff's frown. "Ready?"

Griff squeezed her hand gently and led her out the lodge's front door. They settled into the truck and left Lost Valley Ranch.

Rachel stared at the road ahead, her thoughts going a million miles an hour. "I have the feeling that one of these guys is our killer."

"Is that your gut speaking or wishful thinking?"

Rachel shot him a crooked smile. "Both?"

Griff nodded. "Let's hope you're right."

The ride into Manitou Springs was quick as it was situated between Fool's Gold and Colorado Springs on the downward side of Ute Pass.

"Should we contact Trent's parole officer first?" Griff asked.

Rachel shook her head. "He lives with his parents. They might know where he was the day my sister died, and the day Christy was murdered."

Twenty minutes after they'd left Lost Valley Ranch, they pulled up to a nice little cottage with bold teal exterior paint and a bright yellow door.

Griff and Rachel approached the door and rang the doorbell.

"Hang on, I'm coming," a female voice called out from inside.

A moment later, a woman with a shock of white hair answered the door, a paintbrush in hand.

"Can I help you?" she asked, her gaze going from Griff to Rachel.

"Are you Mrs. Morris?" Griff asked.

"Yes," the woman responded.

"Ma'am, we would like to ask you a few questions about your son, Trent."

She immediately turned away, her friendly smile gone. "If you're here to accuse him of a crime he didn't commit, please leave." Tears slid down her cheeks. "My boy has been through a lot. No man should be treated as he was."

"I'm sorry for your son," Rachel said. "I was

wondering if you might know some of your son's whereabouts at different periods of time."

"Why should I do this?" the woman asked, her chin lifting in challenge.

Rachel smiled softly. "We're trying to recreate a crime scene and rule out people who could not have been there because they were somewhere else."

Mrs. Morris gave a doubtful twist of her eyebrows. "I'll do the best I can. Let me start by telling you my Trent works Monday, Tuesday Wednesday, Thursday and Friday. He's been working that same early-morning shift at the same job since he got out of jail. He hasn't taken off a single day or called in sick. On the weekends, he's with us. Sometimes, our little family goes out for a meal or a weekend trip somewhere fun. What date did you have in mind?"

"Two dates," Rachel said. "All we need to know is where he was on those dates and if someone could vouch for him that day."

Mrs. Morris pulled her cell phone from her pocket and thumbed through the calendar app, stopping on the month Rachel had mentioned. The month in which Lindsay had been killed. The older woman clicked on the day. "Trent would've been working that day. He hasn't asked for a day off since he started work there. You can check with his boss."

Rachel gave Mrs. Morris the other date from fifteen years ago.

"You want me to remember a date from fifteen years ago?" She shook her head, then frowned. "I didn't have those dates saved on my calendar from that long ago. Sorry, I can't help you."

Rachel nodded.

"And for my record," Mrs. Morris said, "My son did not commit rape, though he was convicted on circumstantial evidence of rape of a minor. It wasn't a fair trial from the start. The girl he supposedly raped was his girlfriend. He was nineteen, seeing a sixteen-year-old. They had consensual sex. Her parents were shocked their daughter even knew what sex was. Their daughter didn't want to testify. It was a disaster. My son spent fourteen years in prison for a crime he didn't commit."

"I'm so sorry," Rachel said.

"Are you going to take this little interview and twist it to sell to some news agency?" Mrs. Morris asked, her eyes narrowing.

"No, ma'am," Rachel said.

"Thank you," Mrs. Morris said.

Rachel thanked her and left with Griff.

"We can check with Trent's boss at the feed store to see if he was truly there all day," Rachel said as she climbed into the passenger seat. "I don't think Trent is our guy. I'm not getting any sense of negative juju."

"Since when do you believe in juju?" Griff asked, grinning.

Rachel laughed. "Since I bought some at a craft

fair in Fool's Gold. No, really, Trent isn't our man. We can continue to follow through with his boss, but I'm betting he was working the morning my sister was attacked."

"Next up is Rodney Smith." Rachel read through the one-page description of the man. "Sounds like a big little man, beating on women. His image is murky, but I swear his face is a bit familiar. I just can't place it. We can go to his place and ask him questions. If he's not there, we can swing by his parole officer's office."

She keyed the address into the map app on her smartphone. Within minutes, they pulled up to an apartment complex with many units still under construction. They found the correct unit and walked up to the door.

Griff placed himself between Rachel and the door and tapped his knuckles on the door. They waited a long moment, straining their ears for the sound of footsteps coming their way.

No one answered.

Griff twisted the door handle. It was locked. He peered in through the window and debated breaking into the apartment.

"Are you thinking what I'm thinking?" she asked.

"If you're thinking of breaking and entering, I'm there."

Rachel held out her hand. "Credit card?

He handed her one of his cards and watched how

she slid the card between the door and the door frame. After several attempts, she was able to push the door open into a studio apartment. The place looked barely lived in, with a couple of empty beer cans lying around.

"He's not living here," Rachel said.

She and Griff performed a thorough search of the apartment, finding nothing of interest. No necklaces.

"If he's not living here, where is he living?" Griff asked as they left the apartment, closing the door softly behind them.

"Good question. We should ask his parole officer." She pulled out her cell phone and called the number on the printed sheet. The phone rang several times before going to voicemail.

"He's out of the office until Monday." Rachel settled into the truck and stared down at the image. "I should know this guy, but the name isn't ringing any bells."

"Give it some time. Maybe it'll come to you," Griff said. "Want to grab a bite to eat before we head back to the lodge?"

"Yes, please. I can't believe it's already past noon. While we're waiting for our food, we should call Jake and Thorn to see if they've had any luck."

Griff nodded, pulled out of the parking lot onto the street and headed to the downtown area of Colorado Springs, where he found a café with outside seating.

They sat at a small bistro table, enjoying the view of the mountains.

Rachel ordered a club sandwich.

Griff ordered a Rueben.

After the waiter left to fill their order, Griff called Jake and put him on speaker.

The Navy SEAL answered on the second ring. "Griff, what did you find?"

"Nothing," Griff reported. "Rodney Smith wasn't in his apartment and, apparently, hasn't been there for a while. His parole officer is out of the office until Monday, and we don't have a forwarding address or phone number to track down Smith."

"Great, the man is out on parole, and nobody knows where he is," Jake said. "I'll have Swede search the internet for more photos of Smith that aren't as grainy."

"What about your guys?" Griff asked.

"They had alibis for both dates."

Rachel sighed. "We're back to square one."

"Not yet," Griff said. "We still have to get more information on Smith and find him."

"You two might as well go back to the ranch," Jake said. "I have to stop for supplies; then I'll be back to help gear up for a crazy, busy evening at the Watering Hole."

Griff ended the call and drove out of Colorado Springs up through Ute Pass to Fool's Gold.

"Could we stop by my apartment and the sheriff's office?" Rachel asked.

"Sure," he responded. He drove straight to her apartment complex and parked.

Rachel dropped out of the truck and started toward the stairs to her apartment.

Griff quickly caught up with her.

Rachel used the spare key to open the door and stepped back to allow Griff sufficient room to enter.

Once Griff gave the all-clear gesture, Rachel entered her room and went through her drawers, collecting underwear, another bra and T-shirts. In her closet, she took out another gym bag and stuffed it full of the items she'd need.

"Do you like living here?" Griff asked as they returned to the truck.

Rachel nodded. "In Fool's Gold, yes. In this apartment, not so much. I had a nice house with a yard in San Diego. I hope to have that here someday."

"I like the idea of a little acreage, but not too far out. As long as I'm working, I need quick access to amenities and a decent airport. Jake said working with Brotherhood Protector might mean deploying anywhere in the world."

"Sounds like you're committing fully to Jake's organization." She smiled. "I'm glad."

"I like it here." He reached across the console for her hand and held it for the few seconds it took to reach the sheriff's office.

Inside, Sheriff Faulkner stepped out of his office to greet them. They filled him in on what they'd done so far and their plans for the evening.

"Do you need me to report for duty tonight?" Rachel asked. "I'm perfectly fine."

The sheriff shook his head. "You're not fine. You have a killer after you. I can't have someone trying to kill you and then miss and hit a child. No, stay away from the job until all this dies down."

"Or until I die?" She gave him a twisted grin.

"Don't even say that." The sheriff glared at her. "Focus, woman. I need you back."

She shrugged. "I offered."

"Get out of here." His gaze met Griff's. "Take care of her."

Griff nodded. "I will."

When they left the sheriff's office, Rachel turned to Griff. "I promised to take you to the coffee shop where my sister worked. It closes in a few minutes, but I could use a cup of coffee to see me through a long evening. We can get it to go."

"Lead the way," he said. "I could use some caffeine."

They walked a block and a half down Main Street with traffic steady and busy with tourists streaming in for the Founders Day events. The package delivery van took up several parking spaces in front of the coffee shop. Alan Smith tossed boxes onto a dolly. He glanced up as

Rachel and Griff approached. "Good afternoon," he said.

"Hello, Al. How's your day going?" Rachel asked.

"Couldn't be better." He tossed another box onto the stack. "Attending any of the Founders Day festivities?" he asked.

She shook her head. "Not this year. Got too much going on," she said and stepped into the shop where Lindsay had worked the early morning shift.

"Every time I come in here, I swear I feel her presence," Rachel whispered.

"I wish I had known her," Griff said. "She must have been a very special person."

"She was a free spirit, fiercely independent and loyal." Rachel swallowed hard to dislodge the sudden lump in her throat. "I keep thinking the grief will get easier. So far, it hasn't."

Griff pulled her into his arms, pressed a brief kiss against her lips, and then set her away at arm's length. "You promised me coffee."

She laughed. "I did, didn't I?" They stepped up to the counter and ordered two plain coffees, no sugar or cream.

Al rolled the hand truck into the coffee shop and waited for the manager to sign off on the delivery.

As they waited for their coffee, the shop door opened, and Trent Morris entered, his jeans dusty, his shirt stained with sweat. He took off his ballcap, ran his hand through his hair and slid the cap back over his head. He nodded toward Rachel. "Are you in line?"

Rachel shook her head. "We've ordered."

Griff moved closer, placing his body between Rachel and Trent.

Their names were called out. Griff and Rachel hurried forward to collect their cups and get the hell out of there, passing Trent on their way out.

Once outside, Rachel didn't slow until they reached Griff's truck. She climbed into the passenger seat and finally leaned back.

"I thought you said Trent wasn't the killer?"

She shook her head. "I thought he wasn't. But standing in the coffee shop, I got a weird vibe. Like the killer was there."

CHAPTER 12

THE FURTHER THEY went into the day, the tighter Griff's nerves grew.

The killer had to be planning his move. Griff's gut had never been wrong in the past. Absent? Sometimes, but wrong? No.

Griff and Rachel arrived at the ranch to find more vehicles and people than when they'd left.

More of the Brotherhood Protectors had arrived to help get the lodge and bar decorated, beer iced and food started cooking in the smoker.

As he worked to move tables onto the lawn, Griff introduced himself to several of the former Army Special Operations soldiers who'd helped make Hank Patterson's brainchild come to life in Colorado.

They joked and shared deployment stories. All the while, Griff kept a close eye on Rachel. They ate sandwiches for lunch and shared a big pot of spaghetti for dinner. They did lunch and dinner in shifts to keep a steady number of helpers rotating through the Watering Hole. Already, customers filled the tables and asked for food and drinks.

Griff stood in the doorway between the kitchen and the bar and watched as Rachel weaved between tables, carrying a tray heavy with full drink mugs. When she stopped at a table, she smiled at the customers and distributed the drinks.

Griff manned the bus tubs and cleared tables as quickly as people left. He hadn't done this kind of work since he'd pulled kitchen patrol in the Navy. It could be a thankless job, but fun talking to locals and people who'd come to the festival.

Darkness had descended on the mountain and the valley below. So far, the killer hadn't tried anything and still had his head down.

Enzo Ramos and Thorn helped Gunny in the kitchen, making sandwiches, grilling burgers and hotdogs and frying French fries. RJ and Jake made a helluva team behind the bar, mixing drinks, pouring draft beer and popping the tops off longneck bottles.

Emily, the therapist, and Kayla Quinn worked the tables with Rachel. Tayo Perez and Sawyer parked their big bodies by the front door and crossed their arms over their chests, acting the part of no-nonsense bouncers.

Cage Weaver and Bryce Coleman were on stand-by to drive the drunks home. In the meantime, they cleared tables. Two of the lodge SUVs were parked outside, ready when it was clear a customer wasn't sober enough to get home.

The evening wore on, the room getting louder as more alcohol was consumed.

While cleaning a table on the far side of the room, Griff caught movement out of the corner of his eye near the front entrance. Someone had entered and slipped into the crowd.

A ripple of awareness spread through Griff's body. He straightened and panned the room, searching for the newcomer. He'd made it a point to study every person in the large room. They still didn't know who the killer was, and he hadn't made his move.

Griff did his best to work the tables close to Rachel. He didn't want her too far out of his sight, not in the noisy, packed bar. He doubted he could hear her scream above the cacophony of voices and the jukebox.

Just when he thought it couldn't get louder or rowdier, a shout sounded in the farthest corner of the building. Chairs toppled as men leaped to their feet.

Someone shouted over the roar, "Fight!"

Griff stood tall to peer over the tops of men's heads. Fists flew, and men shouted encouragement to whichever fighter they backed.

Sawyer and Cage waded through the throng,

trying to reach the fist fight that seemed to have grown from two angry people to half a dozen.

As fighters threw their punches, they crashed into the people around them, inciting even more people to join the brawl.

Griff spied Rachel on the other side of the crowd from him. She was working her way through the bystanders to the door leading into the kitchen. She ducked into the kitchen. A moment later, Gunny, Enzo and Thorn ran out and pushed their way through the angry masses.

When Gunny went down, Griff started forward. With the crowd so thick, they might not see a man down. Even as tough as the old fighter was, the Marine could be trampled to death.

Cage and Sawyer urged people to exit the bar. Most resisted, more interested in watching or joining the fight. Their lack of cooperation forced the Protectors to shove people out the door and block them from reentry.

Chairs smashed as people were thrown against them. Men yelled. Bets were made as noses were smashed, and blood made the floor slick.

The noise was deafening.

Griff pushed and shoved his way through the crowd until he reached where Gunny had gone down. He lay on the floor, his arms wrapped around his head to protect himself from stomping boots.

Griff reached for one of Gunny's hands and yanked him to his feet.

"Hold onto my back," Griff said.

Gunny clamped his hands on Griff's shoulders and held on tight as the younger man barged through the crowd that didn't seem to be thinning.

Being bumped and jostled, Griff made painfully slow progress until he finally neared the bar.

RJ lifted the folding countertop and pulled Griff and Gunny into the relative safety behind the bar. As soon as they were inside, RJ slammed the counter down and locked it in place to keep the rabble-rousers from storming the liquor bottles to bash over heads.

Finally able to breathe without having his body crushed against others, Griff drew in a deep breath, clearing his mind so that he could focus.

His first clear thought was, "Where's Rachel?"

"We thought she was with you," RJ said.

"The last I saw her, she was in the kitchen," Gunny said. "She ran in to get us when all hell broke loose out here."

Fuck! Fuck! Fuck!

Griff leaped onto the bar and ran the length to the end closest to the kitchen door. Men stood between him and the door. Griff flung himself into the men, knocking them over like so many bowling pins. He didn't stop to help them to their feet. Instead, he ran across them. With no way to miss the pile of people, he stepped on them as he crossed the space.

Griff made it to the kitchen door and pushed through the swinging door to find opportunists scarfing down the sandwiches Gunny, Enzo and Thorn had made right before the riot had started.

"Did you see a woman with black hair when you came in?" Griff asked.

The men stopped chewing long enough to shake their heads.

Griff raced for the back entrance and slammed through it so hard the door banged against the outside of the building.

"Rachel!" he yelled. Only one person stood in the rear area, close to the edge of the woods surrounding the bar. He bent double and emptied the contents of his belly into the dirt.

Griff ran to him. "Did you see a woman with black hair out here?"

The man shook his head. His eyes rounded, and he clamped a hand over his mouth. He staggered away and barfed again.

A lighted trail led back to the lodge.

Had Rachel gone back to the lodge without telling anyone?

No way. She wouldn't have. Period. She knew how vital it was for her to stay with him.

Griff ran back into the kitchen, grabbed the flash-light from a hook on the wall and raced back out. He shined the light on the dirt beneath his feet, searching for tracks.

Shoe prints disturbed the dust, large feet with treads for hiking.

All he could think was someone had snatched her from the kitchen after Gunny and the others ran in to help stop the fight.

He was certain now that the same person had started the fight as a distraction.

And that person now had Rachel.

RACHEL FADED IN AND OUT. She wasn't sure she was awake. Every time she thought she opened her eyes, all she could see was a pitch-black void.

With each surfacing to consciousness, she grew more and more aware. She lay on her belly, over something hard and loud, her arms trapped against her sides. The air she breathed smelled of dust. Her body heaved right, then left, bumping along as if she were traveling on an unimproved dirt road.

What had happened? Where was she? Where was she being taken?

Her arms and legs were bound. She felt groggy, as if she'd drunk herself into a stupor and couldn't come out of the effects. With no idea how long she'd been out, she also had no idea how far she'd been taken. The sound of the engine indicated some kind of motorcycle or ATV, and she was draped across the legs of its driver.

Slowly, her memory returned, jolted into her head by the roughness of the ride.

She'd run into the kitchen to tell Gunny a fight had broken out and customers were destroying the bar.

Gunny dropped everything and ran for the door, followed by Enzo and Thorn. Gunny slowed long enough to tell Rachel, "Turn off the gas burners."

"I've got this." Rachel moved from burner to burner, twisting the knobs until the gas pilot flickered off. "Go on, keep those construction men from destroying your place."

The three men disappeared behind the swinging door, leaving Rachel alone in the kitchen. By the time she realized her mistake, it was too late. A needle jabbed into her neck, the liquid inside spreading fire into her veins.

Her legs grew weak, and she couldn't lift her arms. As she went down, she thought of Griff.

He'd be beside himself when he realized she was gone.

Unable to move, all of Rachel's promises to herself to fight to the death went out the window. She was entirely at the killer's mercy. She prayed he was taking her a long way to give her time for the drug to wear off so that she could regain her strength.

ELLE JAMES

She could feel the pendent Jake had given her, tapping against her chest with every bump. Rachel prayed Griff and the others would find her before the killer strangled her with a wedding veil. He might add her as his third notch to his belt. But if they could track her, they might catch up to the killer. Please, Lord. If I have to die, make sure they catch the killer before he gets away.

The ATV rumbled to a stop. Her captor slid backward and out from under her, leaving her draped across the seat like a floppy sack of potatoes.

Footsteps sounded behind her. Dark fabric was yanked off her head, and she could see by the light of the stars in the night sky. Still draped over the ATV seat, she couldn't see who was behind her. With her arms still trapped to her sides, she couldn't push herself up.

A sharp point jabbed against her back and ripped through the binding around her arms and body. She moved her arms a little, but not enough to free them from whatever the bind was. It clung to her skin like duct tape.

"Get up," a male voice demanded.

"I can't without the use of my arms."

He grabbed a handful of her hair and yanked her off the four-wheeler and onto her feet.

Rachel swayed. She locked her knees, refusing to succumb to the lingering effects of whatever he'd poisoned her with. She had to find the strength to fight. If she didn't, her life would be over, and the killer would go on to kill again.

She couldn't let that happen. Rachel wanted to live. She had so much more to do in her life to give up now. Number one was to rid the world of this bastard who thought it was his mission to kill women with a wedding veil.

She had to stall him and give Griff and his team a chance to follow her.

Rachel turned to face the killer, shocked to discover Alan Smith standing in front of her, a wedding veil dangling from his fingertips.

"Al? You're the Wedding Veil Killer?" She shook her head. "Why? Why are you doing this?"

He snorted. "You're all the same. Same black hair, same green eyes, same pack of lies."

"What lies, Al?" Rachel asked, working the duct tape loose until it dropped to the ground.

"You flirt and make a man feel like there's hope." His nostrils flared, and his upper lip curled back in a feral sneer. "Then you marry someone else. I'm not good enough, am I, Misty?" He lunged for her, gripped her arms and shook her. "You never loved me, never thought I was good enough for you. You said I was your friend. You said I would always be your friend. You lied, Misty! You lied!"

"Al, listen to me." She met and held his gaze. "I'm not Misty. My name is Rachel. Misty isn't here. She's gone."

"No!" Alan pounded his fist into his palm. "You're standing right in front of me, and you're lying. I know what I see. You can't fool me anymore. I won't let you."

"Al, Misty is gone. You killed her on her wedding day." Every time Alan looked away, Rachel inched backward very slowly. If she could put a little more distance between them, she might succeed at running away from this madman who had killed women he thought were his first love.

She glanced around at the steep mountain trail, bathed in starlight—a rock bluff on one side, a steep slope on the other. She glanced at an incline to her right. It went up another ten feet, and she would bet her lucky rabbit's foot there was a massive drop-off. He'd brought her to the same place where he'd killed Lindsay.

Bastard.

Anger firmed her resolve and gave her the strength she would need to fight. She could not let him get away with another murder.

"You're all alike," he repeated. "You play with a man's affections and then walk away to be with someone else. You don't deserve to marry. You don't deserve happiness when you've destroyed mine, again and again."

"Al, I don't even know you. I've never flirted with you or led you on. I'm not Misty," she said forcefully. "Christy Severs wasn't Misty. She didn't deserve to die. My sister, Lindsay, wasn't Misty. You killed her. Now, I have no family." Her eyes filled with tears and rolled down her face. Rachel scrubbed a hand over her damp cheek. "Listen, Al, we've all been there. We've loved and lost our love to someone else. You can't kill every woman who looks like Misty. It won't bring her back or make her choose you."

"You think I don't know that?" He spat on the ground at her feet. "I'm saving others like me. Saving them the lies and betrayals that destroy your soul."

"No, you're killing them and taking them away from the people who love them," Rachel said. "Misty was an only child. Her parents were devastated. Her fiancé loved her deeply and still misses her. I loved my sister, Lindsay, with my whole heart. She was my only family. And you took her away from me. You can't continue to kill women who look like Misty. It will not fix what is broken inside you."

"See? There you go again, spreading your lies, trying to sway me to your way of thinking. I won't fall for it. I'm done with lies. I'm done with you, Misty. And if you can't love me, you can't love anyone else. You'll only hurt them like you hurt me."

Al lunged toward Rachel.

She dodged to the right, climbing higher to the end of the trail and the deadly drop-off.

What had happened to Lindsay would happen again. This time to her.

If she let it happen.

The hell she would.

Rachel drew on all the self-dense training she'd taken as part of her job as a California State Highway Patrol officer. With a little of the residual effects of the drug he'd injected in her still weakening her muscles, she squared her shoulders and looked for ways to best him that didn't take brute strength.

"You know you can't escape. None of you could. You're weak; I'm strong. You should've chosen me." Again, he lunged toward her. This time, he snagged her arm.

She let him drag her toward him, then she dug in her heels and resisted with all her might.

He leaned backward, using his strength to pull her to him.

Rachel suddenly changed directions and threw all her weight at Al. He'd been leaning back so hard that when she shoved him, he fell backward and released her arm to break his fall.

Free of his grip, Rachel leaped over him and ran down the path, past the ATV, gravity helping her to move faster and faster until she was on the verge of losing control. If she tripped and fell, she'd slide on the gravel, right over the side of the trail and down a slope so steep, she'd pitch and tumble, breaking every bone in her body. She'd die, and Alan would live to kill another day.

Rachel tried to slow her descent. She couldn't run away. She had to stand and fight. She had to finish this, or others would die. In her dream, she'd pushed him over the edge of the trail. If she couldn't subdue the man, she'd throw everything she had at him and send him to hell.

Rachel managed to slow to a stop, her breathing coming in ragged gasps so loud she couldn't hear anything else. She held her breath and listened. For a moment, all she heard was silence. Then a motor revved and raced down the hill toward her.

The trail was too narrow. She wouldn't be able to dodge him without falling over the edge.

Once again, she took off running, searching for a position where she could stand and defend herself. She had to find it soon, or it wouldn't matter. He'd catch up to her and either run her down to kill her or hit her hard enough that she wouldn't be able to run. Then he'd strangle her with his signature wedding veil.

Rachel ran hard. She ran for her life.

CHAPTER 13

"SHE'S GONE," Griff shouted over the continued insanity of the barroom fight.

Jake broke free of the crowd and raced toward Griff at the kitchen entrance. "Was she wearing the necklace we gave her?"

"I don't know. I think so."

Griff turned with Jake and ran out the back door, down the lighted path and into the lodge.

All the way down into the basement, Griff thought, *We're wasting time. We're wasting fucking time. Jesus, man. Every second counts.*

Jake went straight to the cabinet where the tracking device was stored, grabbed it and ran back up the stairs, Griff on his heels, ignoring the pain in his leg the running had caused.

Once they were in the kitchen, Jake waited for the device to warm up and locate the pendent.

Griff held his breath, praying she'd worn it, knowing the killer would make his play.

"There!" Jake pointed at the blue dot on the screen, which displayed a contour map of the area with the streets and roads snaking through.

"They're headed up to the old Merriweather Drop-off," Jake said.

"How do we get there?" Griff asked.

"Follow me." Jake took off running, passing through the dining room, great room and out onto the porch and down the steps.

Griff leaped past the steps, landing hard on his bad leg, and raced after Jake, headed for the barn.

Jake's prosthetic leg didn't slow him down. Griff struggled to keep up.

By the time he found Jake in the barn, his new boss had a four-wheeler revved and waiting.

Jake slipped off the machine, grabbed a roll of duct tape, hopped onto another ATV and secured the GPS tracking device with a single strip of tape.

Griff released the brake, shifted into drive and pressed the throttle. The ATV shot forward and out of the barn.

Jake burst through the barn door, passed Griff and led the way to one of the gates to a pasture. "I know a shortcut," Jake yelled over the sound of the engines. He slid off his machine, opened the gate and jumped back on.

Griff drove his bike through and hopped off to

close the gate behind them. He flung himself onto the ATV and raced to catch Jake.

They drove over hills, down into valleys and across narrow goat trails, clinging to the sides of treacherously steep mountainsides.

The entire time, Griff's heart pounded, and his palms sweated. Would they get there in time? Sweet Jesus, he hoped so. The killer had a head start on them. With Jake's shortcut, Griff hoped they'd arrive before the killer had time to strangle Rachel.

Griff wished he could see the GPS tracker to understand just how much further they had to go to find Rachel.

Jake flew on the back of his four-wheeler, the machine an equalizer for a man with a prosthetic leg and another with a damaged leg.

They zigzagged around the base of the mountain, located the trailhead and climbed the narrow path at dangerously high speeds. There were no guard rails up there. If Griff ran off the road, it was all on him if he survived or died. He focused on the narrow path, refusing to die today. He had to keep the love of his life from death.

Jake slowed and pulled to a stop before a giant outcropping of solid stone.

Griff pulled up beside him and looked at the tracker.

"She's on the other side of this rock formation," Jake said.

"Are we going in on foot or wheels?" Griff asked, anxious to get to her.

Jake responded, "ATV. If he has one, we'll never catch him on foot."

Jake took point with the GPS tracker. As he started around the giant boulder outcropping, a figure shot around the corner, running.

Rachel.

No sooner had she gone around the bend in the trail than an ATV whipped around the rock formation, skidding sideways on loose gravel.

"Rachel!" Griff called out, relieved to see her alive and trying to stay that way.

Jake's ATV leaped forward, blocking the killer's ATV from pursuing Rachel.

Griff hit the throttle and raced toward Rachel.

The killer spun and came at Jake head-on, with no sign of backing down. Jake raced toward him. They played a deadly game of chicken, the killer and the head of the Colorado Division of Brotherhood Protectors.

Griff slowed as he approached Rachel. He held out his arm.

She grabbed it and swung herself up behind him.

Jake held steady until the very last second when he broke left. At the same time, the killer broke to his left. They circled away from each other, the killer heading toward Griff and Rachel.

"Don't let him get away," Rachel yelled over the sound of the engine.

"I can't pursue with you on the back."

The killer blew past them and raced down the trail.

"Go! Go! Go!" she said. "I'll hold on."

Against his better judgment, Griff sped after the killer.

Jake passed Griff, caught up with the ATV ahead of him, passed at a wide spot and swerved to cut him off.

The killer's ATV spun in the gravel, executed a hundred and eighty-degree turn and headed straight for Griff and Rachel.

Griff couldn't remove either hand from the handlebar without crashing into the mountain or over a cliff. "Get my gun!" Griff shouted.

Holding tightly around Griff's belly with one hand, Rachel slid her other hand beneath his leather jacket and snagged his Glock.

Griff hit the brakes and turned the handlebar, making the ATV slide sideways.

Rachel took the shot, the report loud in Griff's ears.

He couldn't see if her one shot had been successful. Like a slow-motion movie, the ATV kept sliding in the gravel in a long, slow curve.

When Griff was able to steer out of the spin, he turned to face their adversary.

The killer's ATV stood in the middle of the trail.

"Where did he go?" Rachel asked, the gun aimed at the killer's ATV.

Griff eased forward.

Jake raced toward them on his four-wheeler.

A shadow rose from the other side of the killer's ATV.

"Look out!" Jake yelled. "He's got a gun!"

Griff hit the throttle.

Gunfire rang out.

Another sounded a split second later.

Pain sliced through Griff's arm as he whipped the ATV around.

In the middle of the turn, the arm around Griff's waist loosened, and Rachel tilted, carried in the centrifugal force of a spinning vehicle.

Griff's arm shot out, catching Rachel before she fell.

Jake circled back, brought his ATV to a halt and jumped off. He squatted beside the man on the ground and touched two fingers to the base of his throat. "Target eliminated."

Griff eased his four-wheeler to a stop with one hand and got off, careful to keep Rachel from falling.

Slipping his arm around her back, he lifted her off the ATV and laid her on the ground. His arm throbbed but wasn't so damaged he couldn't use it. His arm...his leg...didn't matter. What mattered was the woman lying so still on the ground.

"Rachel," he said aloud. He touched her shoulder and felt his way around her in the shadows, searching for the blood. He found the wound on her left side. Blood drenched her shirt and jeans and dripped onto the ground. He shed his jacket, pulled off his T-shirt and folded it into a thick pad. He used it to apply pressure to the wound. "Sweetheart, talk to me."

The starlight illuminated her pale face and her weak smile. "Did we get him?"

"Sweetheart, *you* got him."

She closed her eyes. "For Lindsay."

"That's right. The bastard won't hurt another woman, thanks to you."

"He almost got me."

Griff didn't want to tell her that he had gotten her. His heart clenched as he held the T-shirt to the wound to contain the loss of blood.

"I couldn't let him...get...away," she said, her voice fading to a whisper. "And I wanted to see you...again."

"He's gone now. We can get back to living. You. Me. We can quit pretending. We can make it real." He leaned over her and pressed his lips to her temple. "I love you, Rachel. You make my life worth living in so many ways."

"Love you," she whispered without opening her eyes.

"Rachel?"

She didn't respond.

"Jake! Where's the helicopter? We need to get her to a hospital. Now." His voice broke, and tears slipped down his cheeks. "I can't lose her."

"I've notified 911 and called in a couple of favors with a medical flight organization. They're on their way. Should be here soon."

"I hope it's soon enough," Griff said. "Please, let it be soon enough."

"I also called the lodge. Thorn and Gunny are headed this way. They'll contact someone to collect the body."

That body could rot in hell for all Griff cared. The man had almost killed Rachel.

Jake positioned all three of the four-wheelers to point their headlights at Rachel's position.

Griff checked her pulse and her breathing again and again.

A few precious minutes later, the thumping sound of rotors echoed against the hillside.

A spotlight shone down on them. As the helicopter hovered overhead, a flight medic came down on a cable, carrying a medical equipment case. He sent the cable back up. While the medic worked with Rachel, the cable came down again. This time with a basket attached.

Griff knelt on the other side of Rachel, still applying pressure to the wound while the medic established an IV.

They quickly transferred her to the basket, and

the cable pulled her up into the aircraft, coming back down for the medic.

Gunny and Thorn arrived as the spotlight blinked out and the helicopter rose into the night sky.

Jake spoke briefly to Thorn and Gunny, then yelled, "Let's go!"

Griff hopped onto an ATV and followed Jake back down the trail and all the way to the lodge.

RJ was waiting with Jake's truck running.

The two men left the ATVs in front of the lodge and jumped into the truck.

RJ drove, exceeding the speed limits but carefully negotiating the curves through Ute Pass.

Jake found out which hospital the helicopter would take Rachel. They blew into Colorado Springs thirty minutes later and went straight to the hospital's emergency room.

Rachel had arrived and been wheeled directly to the operating room, where a doctor had been on standby.

Griff, Jake and RJ had nothing else to do but wait.

Griff paced the length of the OR's waiting room several times before his leg started aching. He sat in a chair, buried his face in his hands and prayed for the first time since his entire team had died.

. . .

Sunlight warmed Rachel's face. She shouldn't be lying in bed. Wasn't she supposed to be on day shift today?

Her eyelids fluttered open to bright sunshine streaming through a window she didn't recognize.

"Hey," a voice beside her said.

She turned to see Griff leaning close to her, with dark circles beneath his eyes and thick stubble on his chin.

"Where?" she asked, her voice no more than a croak.

His lips twisted. "In the hospital in Colorado Springs."

Her brow furrowed.

"You were shot," Griff said.

"I thought I shot Al."

"You did. He fired at the same time. You just happened to catch the bullet."

"Oh. Well, hell."

He chuckled. "The OR doc got you all fixed up. You should have a full recovery."

"How long do I have to stay here?" she asked.

"Until you feel up to leaving and the doctor signs off."

"I feel up to leaving." Rachel tried to sit up. Pain shot through her abdomen. She fell back against the hospital bed.

"Hey, you just had surgery." He brushed back a

strand of her hair from her forehead. "Give yourself a little time to recuperate."

"I hate hospitals," she groused.

"I appreciate this hospital, the OR doc and the flight medics who got you here in time."

She grimaced. "Was it that bad?"

He reached for her hand. "You lost a lot of blood."

She liked how strong and warm his fingers were. "How long have I been here?"

"One night," he said.

"When did you get here?"

"Shortly after they flew you in last night."

She stared up at him. "We got him."

He nodded. "You did. He won't hurt anyone ever again."

She closed her eyes and squeezed his hand. "Thank God."

She raised the hand he was holding and brought it to her lips. "Thanks for coming after me. I wouldn't have made it without you."

He grinned. "You were doing a pretty good job of running away from him."

"I wasn't going to let him kill me. I had to live to take him down. And we were right. He was there among us all along. Alan Smith, our package delivery guy. Someone everyone knew." She sighed. "It's scary what we don't know about each other."

"It's not scary what I know about you," Griff said, bringing her hand to his lips to brush a kiss across the backs of her knuckles. "You're strong, brave and loyal. And you don't give up. No matter what. That's what I love about you."

Her heart skipped a beat at his mention of love.

"You know, now that the killer is dead, I won't need a bodyguard," she said. The idea made her sad. "I'll miss having you around."

"You won't have to miss me," Griff said. "I'm not going anywhere."

"No?" Joy made her lips spread into a smile. "That's good news. Are you staying on with the Brotherhood Protectors?"

He nodded. "I am. And I'm staying in Colorado."

She grinned. "You like it here, huh?"

"No. I like it here with you."

Her chest swelled. "And here I thought I was just the job to you."

"Never," he said. "You're everything to me. And it took almost losing you to realize just how much everything meant. I want to be with you always. I love you, Rachel West."

Her eyes filled. "It's a good thing," she said. "Because I've kinda gotten used to having you around. I've never been in love before, but I'm pretty sure this is it."

"Just pretty sure?"

Her hand squeezed his. "You make my knees tremble, and my heart beats faster when you're around."

He cupped her cheek. "Your face is the first one I want to see when I wake up in the morning and the last one I want to see before I go to sleep at night."

Rachel leaned her face into his palm. "What do you say to getting to know each other better when we're not racing against time or being chased by a killer?"

"I'd like nothing better."

"Same," she sighed. "Now, help me up. I want to get started on the part about getting to know each other better."

"Hold on, tiger," Griff laid a hand on her arm to keep her from getting out of the bed. "We'll have plenty of time to make that happen—after you recuperate."

She frowned. "I've never been patient when I've made up my mind what I want. Can I at least have a kiss?"

He laughed, gathered her gently in his arms and kissed her until her heart sang.

Yeah, this was the man for her.

EPILOGUE

"Hey, Griff, did you get the barbeque sauce?" Gunny called out from the grill.

"Yes, sir." Griff hurried down the front porch steps of the lodge and handed over the bottle of sauce. "Smells good."

"Barbeque ribs." Gunny drew in a deep breath. "I think I like them even better than steak. And I like steak a lot. I'm glad to see Rachel up and about. We were all worried about her that night."

"She's strong and stubbornly determined," Griff said. "I have to keep reminding her to slow down and let her insides heal."

"We have a lot of strong-minded women around here. Can't tell 'em anything," Gunny said. "Still can't get over the fact it was Alan Smith who was the killer among us."

"Rodney Alan Smoot," Rachel said as she joined

them at the grill. "He had a lot of people fooled, including his parole officer. And strong-minded isn't a bad thing."

Gunny chuckled. "Heard that, did you?"

"Uh-huh." Rachel smiled at the old Marine.

"It's good to close several cold cases and let all their families heal," Emily said from the porch swing.

"It takes a team to figure it all out," Cage said.

"Couldn't have done it without Rachel, Griff, our guys here and Hank's guys in Montana," Sawyer noted.

Rachel nodded. "I'd been working on it for three months, making no progress."

"Even the Colorado Springs Police Department and State Police couldn't figure it out," Enzo said.

Rachel smiled up at Griff. "I got lucky when Griff pulled me out of the wreckage—and when he and Jake got to me before Alan could finish me off." She glanced around at the men of the Brotherhood Protectors. "You have an amazing, supportive team of men and women. I'm happy to know you're right here if I need you in my duties in the sheriff's department."

"You're going to keep working for the sheriff?" Emily asked.

Rachel nodded. "I'm a cop. I protect my community, whether it's in San Diego or Fool's Gold. It's who I am. Besides, Sheriff Faulkner needs me. They're shorthanded."

"How are those ribs coming?" Jake asked as he stepped out onto the porch, carrying a covered pot. "I've got the baked beans. RJ's coming with the potato salad, and Thorn has the coleslaw." He placed the beans on the middle picnic table of the three they'd put together on the lawn. "Did I hear you talking about Alan Smith?"

"You did," Gunny said.

"Thorn and I met with Misty Lantz's family and found out Alan had dated her for a while. She'd dumped him when he got too possessive and wanted to tell her who she could or couldn't talk to. He followed her around so much that her father had to have a talk with him. They were glad to hear that he'd confessed to killing their daughter and that he won't be around to hurt anyone else."

Rachel leaned into Griff. "We spoke with Christy's folks today. They were glad to finally know the truth and have closure on their daughter's death. It doesn't bring her back but knowing what happened and who did it helped them to understand."

"And the best part is that Alan won't hurt anyone ever again," RJ said as she descended the steps carrying a large bowl.

Gunny plucked the ribs off the grill and laid them on a large platter. "Ribs are ready. Let's eat."

The team gathered around the tables, sliding onto the benches.

"I'd like to make a few announcements before we eat."

Everyone turned to Jake.

Griff knew about one of those announcements, and he was happy Jake was going to make it.

"First," Jake said. "I'd like to officially welcome Griff to the team. After successfully completing his first assignment, he's firmly convinced this is the place he wants to be."

Everyone at the table clapped and cheered.

Griff's cheeks heated, and his heart warmed. He'd lost his team in Syria but gained another in Fool's Gold, Colorado. He knew one could not replace the other, but he had a family again. Brothers.

And he had Rachel.

"Second," Jake continued, "we have a recruit to the Brotherhood arriving next week, fresh from retirement. Former Delta Force Levi Franks."

"I've heard of him," Thorn said.

Cage nodded. "Me, too. He was a legend in Iraq and Afghanistan."

"I worked with him on a joint operation with the Navy SEALs and the Army Deltas," Sawyer said. "He'll be a good addition to the team."

"Last and certainly not least," Jake smiled over at RJ, whose cheeks flushed a bright red, "RJ and I are going to have a baby." He shot a glance at Gunny. "The wedding will be in a month's time. You're all invited."

A rowdy cheer went up around the table.

Griff pounded Jake on the back, grinning from ear to ear. "So happy for you, man." His heart was full for his new boss and friend.

He turned to Rachel, took her hand in his and squeezed it gently. Yes, he'd found a new home and family.

"I love this team," Rachel said beside him. "They feel like family."

He chuckled. "I was thinking the same thing. With you and the Brotherhood Protectors, I have a family."

Rachel leaned into his shoulder. "That's how I feel as well. I'm glad you're staying. You fill me with hope for happiness."

"Sweetheart, being with you fills my heart with more joy than I thought I'd ever find after all the tragedy I've witnessed." He leaned over and planted a kiss on her lips.

Rachel stared up into his eyes and whispered for his ears only, "I love you, John Griffin."

"I love you, too, Rachel West."

SAVING KYLA

BROTHERHOOD PROTECTORS
YELLOWSTONE BOOK #1

New York Times & USA Today
Bestselling Author

ELLE JAMES

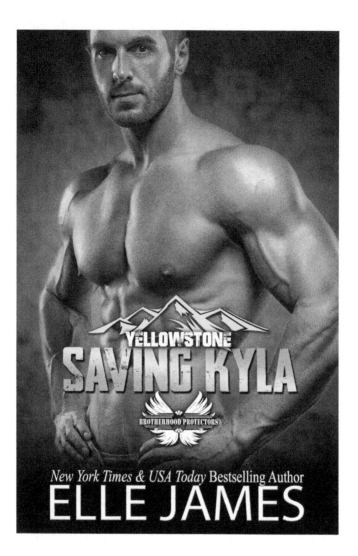

YELLOWSTONE
SAVING KYLA

BROTHERHOOD PROTECTORS

New York Times & USA Today Bestselling Author
ELLE JAMES

CHAPTER 1

KYLA RUSSELL WAS DONE with killing.

Especially when her target didn't deserve to die.

Camouflaged as an Afghan male in a long white thobe, the ankle-length white shirt Afghan men wore, she stood on a street in Kandahar, Afghanistan, a pistol with a silencer attached strapped to her thigh. Beneath the thobe, she wore dark jeans and a dark shirt for night movement.

She'd pulled her long, black hair up and wrapped it in a dark turban like the ones worn by men in the city. To complete her disguise, she'd applied a fake beard, bushy eyebrows and dark makeup to make her appear more masculine and able to walk freely around the city of over six hundred thousand people.

Kyla had spent the better part of the day before studying her target, both through the windows of his home and by tailing him as he'd left for work and returned. What about this man made him toxic? Why had her government deemed him dangerous to the world?

She made it a priority to research her assignments, to find out about the persons she was assigned to eliminate. Prior to accepting her current mission, she'd reviewed the dossier her handler had given her for Abdul Naser Ahmadi and had done her own background check on the man via her connections on the internet and the Dark Web.

The dossier had listed Ahmadi as an arms trafficker, supplying American weapons to the Taliban. Nothing in Kyla's own research indicated the same. In fact, Ahmadi was like a black hole of information. All she could find was that he lived with his wife in Kandahar and worked at a local university as a professor of language and literature.

Kyla had no qualms about ridding the world of pedophiles or people who tortured and killed others for their race or religious beliefs. She'd taken out cult leaders who'd planned terrorist activities in the United States and some who were killers in foreign countries.

Some of her targets had been dirty politicians, selling secrets to US enemies, placing her country's military in jeopardy. Those targets, she'd taken out with no problem and no regrets. The world was a better place without them.

Kyla took pride in never completing a mission

without first understanding the target and the necessity of taking him out.

Ahmadi was not raising any red flags. Still, she planned to observe the man for a couple of days in case she was wrong.

Standing on a street corner, her back to the wall of a building, she casually observed Ahmadi at a local tea shop where he sat with another man. Maybe this was the reason for the hit—this meeting with Ahmadi's guest.

Using her cellphone, Kyla snapped a picture of the man and sent it to her contact on the Dark Web, who had access to facial recognition software.

Within minutes she was surprised to receive a response.

Jalal Malik CIA.

Kyla frowned at the message. *CIA? What the hell?*

Kyla sent the picture of Malik and Ahmadi along with a message to an old friend she'd known from her days in the CIA. A man who had access to more than he should.

Jalal Malik CIA...Legit? Clean?

Her contact responded several minutes later:

Born in the US to first-generation Afghans who escaped Afghanistan and Taliban rule thirty years before and earned their US citizenship. Malik speaks fluent Pashto and joined the CIA to give back to the country that saved his parents. Now working to uncover a mole in the US government, who is feeding information and arms to the Taliban. Ahmadi is his trusted informant.

With Ahmadi in her sights, Kyla could have picked him off any time that day and disappeared. However, she couldn't pull the trigger, not when her gut told her something was off. Ahmadi wasn't dangerous to the US. In fact, his willingness to help the US find the traitor within made him an asset and put him in danger of Taliban retaliation. Why had he been targeted for extermination?

She'd followed him home to ask him that question. By the time he'd returned to his home, darkness had settled over Kandahar.

Kyla ducked into the shadows of the wall surrounding Ahmadi's home, where she stripped out of the white thobe and trousers and tucked them behind a stack of stones. Then she pulled herself up and over the wall, dropped down into Ahmadi's yard and watched for her chance to corner the target.

That chance presented itself within the hour.

Ahmadi's wife had gone to the bedroom. Ahmadi stepped out his back door onto the hardpacked dirt within the stone wall to smoke a cigarette.

Kyla slipped up behind him, clamped her hand over his mouth and pressed a pistol with the silencer attachment to his temple. She lowered her voice and spoke in Pashto, "Tell me why my government wants you dead."

He stood still, making no attempt to fight back. "Who is your government?"

She nudged his temple with the pistol. "The same government who sent your guest at tea."

He nodded and switched to English. "Perhaps we are getting too close to the truth," he said in a whisper.

Kyla released the man and stepped back, her weapon trained on Ahmadi's chest as he turned to face her, his hands raised.

"I am not your enemy," he said.

"Then why would my government send me to kill you?" she asked.

He shook his head. "For the same reason I had tea with another citizen of your country. One of your own is playing for the other side and has sent you to do his dirty work."

"What do you know that would make someone put a hit out on you?" she asked.

"If you will not kill me, I will tell you what I told my guest at tea." Ahmadi's eyes narrowed as he awaited her response.

Kyla lowered her weapon. She could still kill him if he made a move to hurt her.

Ahmadi drew in a deep breath and let it out slowly before speaking again. "I received the name of the man who has been coordinating shipments to the Taliban. He goes by...Abaddon."

"Abaddon?"

The man nodded. "The meaning of the name is destruction."

At that moment, Ahmadi's wife called out in Pashto, "Are you expecting a delivery? A van just arrived in front of our gate."

Ahmadi glanced toward the house.

A knot of foreboding formed in Kyla's gut. "Call your wife to you."

Ahmadi frowned. "Why?"

"Just do it. Now." Kyla turned and slipped between the wall and the house.

Behind her, Ahmadi called to his wife.

Through the windows, Kyla could see Ahmadi's wife moving toward the back of the house.

Kyla slowed at the front corner and peered through the wrought iron gate at a dark van parked on the street. A door opened, and a man dressed in dark clothes and a ski mask dropped down.

If the mask wasn't enough to make her blood run cold, the mini machine gun he carried did the trick.

Kyla's pulse slammed through her veins. She spun and raced to the back of the house, where Ahmadi and his wife stood together.

Kyla glanced at the wall she'd scaled easily. Ahmadi and his wife would not go over it as quickly, dressed as they were in long robes.

In Pashto, she said, "Over the wall. Hurry." She bent and cupped her hands.

Ahmadi urged his wife to go first.

She hung back.

"Go," Kyla urged. "Or we all die."

The woman stepped into Kyla's palms. With her husband pushing from behind, she landed on her stomach and swung her leg over the top of the stone wall. She dropped to the other side.

Kyla held her hands for Ahmadi.

"No, you go first," Ahmadi said.

"No time to argue," she remained bent over.

Ahmadi stepped into her hands.

Kyla straightened.

Ahmadi pulled himself up to the top of the wall and reached down to give her a hand up.

She shook her head. "Go!"

He slipped over the wall and dropped to the ground on the other side.

Doors slammed open inside the house as the man in the black ski mask worked his way through the rooms. It wouldn't take him long. The house wasn't that big.

Kyla got a short, running start, scaled the wall and slung her leg over.

As she slipped over the top, she glanced back. The man in the black ski mask had just reached the back door and flung it open. Before he could see her, she dropped to the other side.

Her turban caught on a crack in the wall. Unable to stop and free it, she let it go, the ponytail she'd wound around her head shaking loose. She didn't have time to retrieve her thobe. It didn't matter. Without the turban, the disguise was useless. All she could do was run. She raced after Ahmadi and his wife.

They ran for several city blocks. The couple wouldn't be able to keep up the pace for long.

Kyla glanced over her shoulder. The man in black rounded a corner and sprinted toward them.

"Turn left," Kyla yelled to the couple. They did, and Kyla followed. "Keep going and find a safe place to hide. I'll take care of him." She stopped running and waited for the assassin to catch up.

Ahmadi and his wife turned another corner, zigzagging through the streets.

Kyla waited, her gun poised and ready. When the man didn't burst around the corner as she expected, she eased her head around.

Several yards away, the man was climbing into the van's passenger side. Once he was in, the van leaped forward, headed for her corner.

Kyla aimed at the driver's windshield and fired.

Her bullet pierced the window.

The van swerved and then straightened, coming straight for her position on the corner.

She fired again.

This time the van swerved and slid sideways into a building.

The man in the ski mask jumped out of the

passenger side and, using the door for cover, aimed his rifle at Kyla.

Knowing her pistol didn't have the range or accuracy of the shooter's rifle, she backed away from the corner and ran. She had to get to a better position to defend herself or get the hell away.

She was halfway to the next corner when tires squealed behind her.

A glance over her shoulder confirmed...the van was back in action and barreling toward her.

In front of her, headlights flashed as a small sedan turned onto the street. A man leaned out of the passenger window with a rifle and fired at her.

Fuck.

The bullets hit the pavement beside her. Kyla turned right onto the street nearest her and ducked behind the first home she came to. She circled the house, leaping over piles of stones and brick, and hid in the shadows near the rear of the home as the sedan turned onto the street. The van was slowing as it approached the corner.

As the van turned, Kyla aimed at the front tire of the van and popped off a round. The tire blew and sent the van veering toward the front of the house behind which she hid and crashed into the front entrance.

Kyla didn't wait for the driver to recover. She backtracked and ran back in the direction from which she'd come, zigzagging between houses, hugging the shadows as she went. Several times, she was certain she glimpsed the sedan.

She hoped Ahmadi and his wife had made good their escape. After she'd split from them, she was certain the attackers had been after her. They had to know she wasn't Ahmadi. Her long ponytail would have given her away.

Making her way through the darkened streets, she pulled off the fake beard and eyebrows, wincing as the glue proved stubborn. She couldn't stay in Kandahar. Not dressed as she was. The Taliban patrolled the streets day and night, looking for people breaking the newly enforced laws. She would be arrested or beaten for her lack of appropriate attire.

Not knowing exactly who the attackers were, she couldn't afford to be caught. If they were members of the elite team of assassins she was a part of, they would know they were chasing her—and they were aiming for her, specifically.

As of that moment, she no longer worked for the US government. She was now a threat to the people who'd trained and recruited her. They'd be looking for her in Kandahar. She no longer had the support to get her out of the country. If she wanted out, she'd have to find her own way.

Double fuck.

Kyla made her way to the edge of the city, moving quickly. She had to get out before sunrise. She couldn't trust anyone. People wouldn't be willing to help her. Not a lone female without male protection. Especially dressed as a Westerner in pants, not wearing the mandated black abaya.

As she arrived on the edge of the city, she paused in the shadows of a fuel station.

A truck pulled up, loaded with bags of onions, oranges and various other produce. From the direction it had come, it was heading out of town for an early morning delivery.

Kyla waited for the driver to fill his tank and pay the attendant.

When he finally climbed back into the cab and started his engine, Kyla made her move.

The truck pulled out from beneath the light from a single bulb hanging over the pump and slowly picked up speed on the road heading west.

Kyla glanced left and then right.

The attendant had returned to the inside of the station. No other vehicles were in sight.

She took off, sprinting after the truck, grabbed the side rail and vaulted up into the back, landing on a stack of bagged oranges. Adjusting several heavy bags, she created a hole and fit herself into the middle, out of sight of other traffic that might pass them on the road. She settled back, praying when they stopped that she could find a way out of Afghanistan and back to the States.

Once there, she'd use her nefarious contacts in

the Dark Web and her former colleagues in the CIA to find out what the hell had just happened.

THE BUMPY ROAD and the sway of the old vehicle must have lulled her to sleep.

When the truck slowed and made a couple of sharp turns, Kyla's eyes blinked, and she stared up at the sun beating down on her and the buildings on either side of the truck as it maneuvered into a small village at the edge of the hills. She guessed it was making a delivery stop, which meant she needed to get out before the driver brought the truck to a complete stop.

Kyla pushed the bags of oranges out of the way and scooted toward the tailgate. As the truck turned another corner, she dropped out of the back and rolled in the dust into the shadows, coming to a stop when she bumped up against a pair of boots.

ABOUT THE AUTHOR

ELLE JAMES also writing as MYLA JACKSON is a *New York Times* and *USA Today* Bestselling author of books including cowboys, intrigues and paranormal adventures that keep her readers on the edges of their seats. When she's not at her computer, she's traveling, snow skiing, boating, or riding her ATV, dreaming up new stories. Learn more about Elle James at www.ellejames.com

Website | Facebook | Twitter | GoodReads | Newsletter | BookBub | Amazon

Or visit her alter ego Myla Jackson at mylajackson.com
Website | Facebook | Twitter | Newsletter

Follow Me!
www.ellejames.com
ellejamesauthor@gmail.com

ALSO BY ELLE JAMES

Shadow Assassin

Delta Force Strong

Ivy's Delta (Delta Force 3 Crossover)

Breaking Silence (#1)

Breaking Rules (#2)

Breaking Away (#3)

Breaking Free (#4)

Breaking Hearts (#5)

Breaking Ties (#6)

Breaking Point (#7)

Breaking Dawn (#8)

Breaking Promises (#9)

Brotherhood Protectors Yellowstone

Saving Kyla (#1)

Saving Chelsea (#2)

Saving Amanda (#3)

Saving Liliana (#4)

Saving Breely (#5)

Saving Savvie (#6)

Two Dauntless Hearts

Three Courageous Words

Four Relentless Days

Five Ways to Surrender

Six Minutes to Midnight

Hearts & Heroes Series

Wyatt's War (#1)

Mack's Witness (#2)

Ronin's Return (#3)

Sam's Surrender (#4)

Take No Prisoners Series

SEAL's Honor (#1)

SEAL'S Desire (#2)

SEAL's Embrace (#3)

SEAL's Obsession (#4)

SEAL's Proposal (#5)

SEAL's Seduction (#6)

SEAL'S Defiance (#7)

SEAL's Deception (#8)

SEAL's Deliverance (#9)

SEAL's Ultimate Challenge (#10)

Texas Billionaire Club

Tarzan & Janine (#1)

Something To Talk About (#2)

Who's Your Daddy (#3)

Love & War (#4)

Billionaire Online Dating Service

The Billionaire Husband Test (#1)

The Billionaire Cinderella Test (#2)

The Billionaire Bride Test (#3)

The Billionaire Daddy Test (#4)

The Billionaire Matchmaker Test (#5)

The Billionaire Glitch Date (#6)

The Billionaire Perfect Date (#7) coming soon

The Billionaire Replacement Date (#8) coming soon

The Billionaire Wedding Date (#9) coming soon

Ballistic Cowboy

Hot Combat (#1)

Hot Target (#2)

Hot Zone (#3)

Hot Velocity (#4)

Cajun Magic Mystery Series

Voodoo on the Bayou (#1)

Voodoo for Two (#2)

Deja Voodoo (#3)

Cajun Magic Mysteries Books 1-3

SEAL Of My Own

Navy SEAL Survival

Navy SEAL Captive

Navy SEAL To Die For

Navy SEAL Six Pack

Devil's Shroud Series

Deadly Reckoning (#1)

Deadly Engagement (#2)

Deadly Liaisons (#3)

Deadly Allure (#4)

Deadly Obsession (#5)

Deadly Fall (#6)

Covert Cowboys Inc Series

Triggered (#1)

Taking Aim (#2)

Bodyguard Under Fire (#3)

Cowboy Resurrected (#4)

Navy SEAL Justice (#5)

Navy SEAL Newlywed (#6)

High Country Hideout (#7)

Clandestine Christmas (#8)

Thunder Horse Series

Hostage to Thunder Horse (#1)

Thunder Horse Heritage (#2)

Thunder Horse Redemption (#3)

Christmas at Thunder Horse Ranch (#4)

Demon Series

Hot Demon Nights (#1)

Demon's Embrace (#2)

Tempting the Demon (#3)

Lords of the Underworld

Witch's Initiation (#1)

Witch's Seduction (#2)

The Witch's Desire (#3)

Possessing the Witch (#4)

Stealth Operations Specialists (SOS)

Nick of Time

Alaskan Fantasy

Boys Behaving Badly Anthologies

Rogues (#1)

Blue Collar (#2)

Cowboy Sanctuary

Lakota Baby

Dakota Meltdown

Beneath the Texas Moon

.

Made in the USA
Las Vegas, NV
19 November 2022

59877246R00144